AF225183

How Much is That Doggie In The Window?
Copyright©2014 Barry Lowe
ISBN 978-1-909934-63-4
Cover art and design by Dawné Dominique

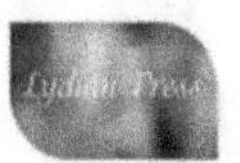

Published by
Lydian Press 2014
Find us on the World Wide Web at
www.lydianpress.com

HOW MUCH IS THAT DOGGIE IN THE WINDOW?

Barry Lowe

Lydian Press

How can anyone resist those eyes?

HOW MUCH IS THAT DOGGIE IN THE WINDOW?

"Ralph Esseltine?" I couldn't believe my ears. "That nasty old codger who gives other old codgers a bad name?"

Trish smirked. She had no love for the old fart either. He was so mean he made Scrooge look like a philanthropist and we're talking here of Scrooge before the visits by the ghosts of Christmases immemorial. "The very same. Megan Hathaway, his cook, rang us concerned about his well-being. We sent one of our community nurses around–"

I interrupted because I knew what was coming. "Don't tell me. He reduced her to tears and she swore she'd never go back?"

"Think again. She was more than eager to return. Said she'd take a rope with her next time and string the old bastard up by his balls."

"If he doesn't want any help, why send me?"

"Megan says it's not physical, it's mental. He lacks for company. No one to talk to."

"I don't think Esseltine does talking. I think his idea of a conversation is to order people around and browbeat anyone who isn't of the same opinion. Relatives?"

Trish consulted the file she had open on her computer. "A grandson is all we have on the record. Esseltine disowned his daughter when she married so the grandson is a no show."

"Her husband was from the wrong side of the blanket of privilege?"

"Yeah. They both...um...died about ten years ago."

"Sad."

"We contacted the grandson but his attitude was, and I quote, 'I hope the old bastard rots in hell.' Seems there's no love lost there."

Esseltine was well-known and well-disliked in the town as well. He owned most of the property in Callicoma's central business district plus a huge swathe of the rainforest to the west of the town which was home to the Black Wattle that gave the town its name. The government had been pressuring the old guy to donate it to the adjoining state forest or, at the very least, leave it to the People in his will. Esseltine's response had been to tell the powers-to-be to 'suck my parched balls' before he'd consider such a thing. If they offered him good money he'd consider it but told them not to come back until they had a serious offer. By serious he meant multi-millions of dollars.

He took no prisoners when it came to financial transactions. Many a farmer in the area had been forced off his land when Esseltine foreclosed by impatiently demanding his mortgage even though the amount owed was so trivial it would not even have been missed.

"That's beside the point," he had informed a journalist who managed to gain entry to his old mansion perched on the tallest hill overlooking the town. Just like its solitary and lonely owner, the house lorded it over the inhabitants of Callicoma, the land around fallow and desiccated because Esseltine had bought it up to ensure no one ever encroached on his privacy. Had the miserable old bastard lived in medieval times he would probably have been burned at the stake as one of Satan's spawn.

"You let one person get away with not paying his debts, then another asks and then another. Soon you'll be in the poor house. When people sign up, they know the rules. A little bit of hardship never hurt anyone" was his credo.

Tell that to the people who've lost their homes or their livelihoods, I thought when I read the newspaper interview. It garnered old Ralph Esseltine no new friends except maybe those with an obsession about accumulating wealth but they kept their mouths tightly shut because if it's one thing the article did gain for the old curmudgeon, it was loads of new enemies.

As a result, absolutely no one cared when Esseltine fell down the floridly designed grand staircase in his mansion and lay in agony until his cook/cleaning lady returned three days later because he was too mean to give her permanent employment. She cooked enough to last the period between visit whenever she was at the mansion, storing it in the fridge for him, marked with a felt pen so he would know which meal to eat. She was expected to dust in her spare time; not that she had any. Esseltine told her, "A house only needs a good clean once a week. If we spent our time attempting to wipe away every speck of dust then we should get nothing done that's important." Important, of course, meant making money.

That fall from the lofty heights was how I met the man for the first time. He was unable to care for himself in the large rambling mansion and he was too frugal to employ a full-time nurse or housekeeper to make his meals and generally watch over his well-being. He had suffered numerous fractures – no one was completely sure how many broken bones as rumor had begun adding to his injuries – and was confined to bed to recover. He ended up as a patient in the local nursing hospital where I volunteer of a weekend, so, it was inevitable that we meet.

I knew of him by reputation although I don't believe I had ever set eyes on him before that first weekend. He was as far outside my circle of friends and business dealings as I was his. I'm the town's veterinarian and, from what I'd heard, it was as likely that Esseltine would have a pet of any description as that pigs might suddenly gain the ability to become airborne. To him, animals, like humans, had to pay their way. The only good thing to be said about furred, hoofed and feathered creatures was they were good on his table at meal time.

Having the emotional life of the chronically unappreciated, I spent my weekends at the local hospital cheering up long-stay and terminally ill patients. In case I've given you totally the wrong impression, I have no skills whatsoever as a stand-up comic, singer, magician, entertainer or player of a musical instrument. I'm rather shy around people. Oh,

I don't dislike them, it's just I'm more comfortable around animals.

It was my original idea that I bring a few of the dogs from my shelter every weekend to help cheer up the sick and suffering. It's amazing what the unconditional love of a small furry bundle yipping and frolicking around the wide expanse of lawn can do for the well-being of patients. And of nursing staff. I mainly brought puppies and kittens that had been abandoned on the front step to my office by anonymous people who had neither the heart nor the cash to care for them properly, or else the various animals delivered to me by welfare groups when they were discovered battered and injured and close to death. What can I say? I'm a soft touch.

Some of the new arrivals were too far gone to survive and those I disposed of as humanely as possible, always with a heavy heart at Man's inhumanity to animals, and always with a tear or two no matter the sheer volume that passed through my surgery every week.

I was lucky that I was supported by Trish Nolan, the nurse-administrator who ran the hospital/nursing home with a steely professionalism when it came to dealing with doctors and anesthetists but which she leavened with an acute sense of humanity when dealing with the patients. That's why she threw her support behind my ideas in the face of indifference or else outright hostility of some members of the Board who ran the hospital.

"They'll come around, Leon," she said when she relayed the provisional okay to my scheme. "They're always conservative when it comes to something new. They'll be your biggest fans when they see the efficacy of your idea."

Indeed, most of them had in time. There were a few conservative elements that were hold-outs but I had little to fear from them as my experiment in animal therapy got results: a happier atmosphere and a vast improvement in the mental and emotional well-being of the patients, even among those whose condition was terminal.

Always careful to choose the most placid of animals because I knew they would be petted and prodded and sometimes handled a little more roughly than usual, albeit unintentionally, by youngsters with more enthusiasm than experience, or older patients with hands deformed by arthritis who mainly clasped one of the fur balls in their laps or against their breasts much too tightly. It was always sad when I had to collect the animals at the end of each Saturday or Sunday as the ill and infirm bid goodbye to their weekend companions.

Some patients formed such strong attachments to their furry friend that they took it home permanently once they had recovered. I let the animals go with great reluctance because I would have selfishly kept them all, given the opportunity. I knew, however, they were going to loving homes where they would be well cared for.

The weekend I met Ralph Esseltine, developing an intense personal dislike for him, was like any other. I turned up as usual with my van emblazoned *Creature Comforts* containing the cheer-up squad watered and fed but not so sated that the patients could not tempt them with treats they'd saved from the kitchen or had purchased from the small convenience store on site. That gave joy on both sides. The patients had been trained as well as the dogs and cats. They knew not to give chocolate or other so-called human treats, no matter how tempting, to their animal friends for the day. Anyone caught disobeying the rules lost companion privileges and I'd seen grown men and women reduced to tears and to begging when they lost their weekend visitor. It broke my heart but the last thing I wanted was a sick animal. The miscreants all learned their lesson and never tried it again.

I was really surprised therefore when I heard one of the dogs whimper in pain and surprise as I was kneeling in the grassy courtyard to release the last of the puppies to gambol among the patients as they pleased. That was my way of allowing each pup and each patient to find a partner to their satisfaction. The new dogs would yap and run from chair to chair, licking hands, faces, anything they could get their tongue to, like young kids let loose in the park. The burst of freedom was too much for some who galumphed around the lawn, never settling down until they fell exhausted on the grass, falling sleep in the warm sun.

Looking up, I noticed Tynan sitting on his haunches, his head downcast but his eyes staring at a man seated in a garden chair, his legs covered in a blanket. The elderly gentleman was wiping his hand with a monogrammed handkerchief. When he'd completed his task he kicked in the direction of the pup although there was no chance of connection as Tynan was out of range, and spat, "Get away from me you filthy little beast." Tynan may have been young but he already understood tone and loped away in search of someone more amenable to his personality.

"Who's that charmer?" I asked Vera Wardrop as I settled Sherlock, a fluffy blue Birman, in her lap. She and Sherlock were devoted to each other and I suspected Sherlock would be going home with Vera at the end of her recuperation.

"That's old man Esseltine," she sneered. "More money than God and less charm than the Devil."

"The rich guy that owns most of the town?"

"The very same," Vera replied. "I'd wish him all the pain in the world but I already know he's suffering. Something terminal, I've been told." She did like a good gossip although, in this case, she'd been misinformed.

I knew Vera's family had suffered at Ralph Esseltine's greedy hands in the past so I expected no less of her; still, it's hard to wish the worst on a fellow human being. I walked over to where Esseltine sat bunched under the blanket on what was a wonderfully warm and sunny day. He must have sensed my presence because, without looking up, he snarled, "Take me back inside this instant."

Putting as much enthusiasm into my voice as I could spare, I said, "It's such a lovely sunny day."

Old Scrooge Esseltine grunted. "I hate the sun. It burns the skin. Gives you wrinkles."

I looked closely at his face. He had no worry about more wrinkles, he already had the appearance of an ageing shar pei. I was tempted to tell him so, but I refrained with much difficulty.

It's not my job to move the patients, in fact, it's frowned upon. I ignored his request. "I'm sorry if Tynan annoyed you," I said.

"Who the fuck is Tynan?" The man seemed incapable of speaking civilly. He snapped or sneered or bellowed or spat.

"The little pup that seemed to displease you."

"Filthy animal. It licked my hand. I'll probably get an infection."

I rose to my full height. "I'll have you know my dogs are as clean as an operating theatre. They've had all their shots, they're bathed regularly—"

He snorted his contempt.

I was indignant, but I should have controlled my temper. "In fact, Tynan is more likely to catch some terrible disease from someone like you than the other way round."

I suspect Esseltine was unused to be spoken to in such a disrespectful manner and he looked up in surprise. "A hospital is no place for wild animals."

I wasn't going to budge one inch now that the old goat had got me riled. "First, my animals are well trained and well behaved, even the pups like Tynan…"

The dog must have heard his name mentioned and trotted over nonchalantly looking for another hand to lick. He looked up at me expectantly, then to Esseltine with a subtle growl.

"Dangerous bloody wild animal," he swore, kicking at the pup that was wise enough to stay out of reach.

Esseltine had grabbed his walking stick and was poking it in Tynan's direction provoking the pup into loud yapping sounds as he snapped his jaws at the stick.

"See," Esseltine gloated. "It wants nothing better than to bite me."

"If someone was poking a stick in your face, I guess you'd want to bite them, too." I'd had enough. Grabbing the walking stick out of his arthritic old hands, I stepped back far enough that I could prod and poke it toward his head forcing him to duck and weave to avoid it although there was no likelihood it would ever reach him. During the diversion, Tynan walked over to Esseltine's blanketed legs, lifted his own leg and pissed copiously all over the old guy's slippers, before trotting away proud of his achievement. "Good boy, Tynan," I called.

A number of other patients who had been watching the confrontation, dared to applaud.

"I'll have your fucking job," he bellowed as he shook his foot in an unsuccessful attempt to dislodge his slipper full of dog piss. "Nurse! Nurse!"

I walked away as a nurse scuttled past giving me a wink which was as good as a high five. I heard her tut loudly as she got to the complaining Esseltine. "Why, Mr. Esseltine," she cried, all mock concern. "If you'd wanted to use the toilet all you had to do was ask and

I would have brought you a bottle. Now you've gone and wet yourself. Oh, dear."

As Esseltine sputtered in indignation, a number of those on the lawn laughed openly. Yep, Ralph Esseltine was definitely one unpopular old man.

As the nurse wheeled him toward the hospice building I heard him ranting that "I'll buy this place and fire the lot of you."

Late in the afternoon as I gathered up the pets to return to the shelter, a number of the patients confided it was the best laugh they'd had in ages.

I didn't expect to escape reprimand because Esseltine had contacts and cronies everywhere, including the Board of the Hospital. Esseltine had been on the phone that very afternoon, I was told, so the boot in the ass made its way from the top through middle management to end up wedged tightly in the butt of Trish Nolan. I sat opposite her attempting to look as contrite as possible and failing miserably.

"I explained to them that they'd have a patient riot on their hands if we stopped you from your weekly visits. I also emphasized that you were doing it at no charge to the hospital. That impressed a few of them. The clincher was when I informed them that when it got out that old man Esseltine was responsible for banning the pets then he was likely to wake up one morning dead with his throat cut. That shook them up a bit."

I couldn't help it, I laughed. "So where does that leave me now?"

"Same as always. We reached a compromise. Mr. Esseltine will use the private courtyard while you're here so that no animals can molest him." Trish couldn't help smirking. When she got herself under control again, she looked at me sternly. "Consider yourself reprimanded, Leon."

"Will you have to spank me?" I teased.

"I suspect you'd like that. Not from me though. Maybe from Bruno?"

Bruno was the exceedingly cute male nurse who was built like a champion wrestler but was straight as an arrow although he knew I had a crush on him and used it to torment me by getting upfront and personal every opportunity he got. He put his arm around my shoulder to hug me to his massive chest. "Got yourself a man yet, Leon?" he'd ask, flicking his fingers across my nipples until I shuddered and had to run to the men's room to relieve the ache in my crotch. Bastard.

At first I thought he was closeted but I found out he was bedding just about every available female nurse on staff plus a few of the married ones as well. He was a classic narcissist; he loved the effect his sculpted body and male model looks had on people, female and male. He especially liked that his body got me hard.

I met him coming out of Trish's office after my carpeting. More like a bath matting really. I was grinning when I felt the familiar weight of Bruno's arm on my back. "Hey, little buddy. I heard you were in deep shit. Everything okay?" He might be a tease but he looked after his own.

"Everything's fine, Bruno. Trish had to give me a bollocking but it was pretty mild."

"That Esseltine is a miserable bastard," he said. "We were gonna put scorpions in his bed if he got you barred from the hospital. You're one popular dude, man."

"Thanks, Bruno."

"When are you gonna find yourself another nice dude and settle down?"

"How can I Bruno? You're the perfect man for me and no one else can ever live up to that."

He flicked my nipples. "Aw, Leon, that's so sweet. Maybe if you get me drunk enough, I'll let you fuck me." With that he winked and sashayed off down the corridor swishing his butt from side to side. My laugh followed him.

I didn't see Esseltine the next few weekends although his presence hung over the hospital like a pall of hazardous waste. Everyone from patients to nurses to administrators seemed tense and irritable. The general consensus seemed to be that they all wished he was gone – preferably in a casket. Yep, he was that popular.

It was a month later that the poisonous atmosphere cleared and when I arrived for my usual Saturday visit, something I had always looked forward to until Esseltine became a patient, the dread in my stomach actually making me wonder whether it was worth the hassle any longer, everyone was in good spirits.

"Did he die?" I asked, none too sensitively.

Trish whispered, "We all wish. But, no, he decided he preferred the comfort of his own home. He can afford to employ a nurse full-time; we don't need him here disrupting our schedule. One of the more sympathetic Board members had a quiet word to him. Seems to have done the trick."

I released the animals from the back of my van and a few of the dogs raced to greet their favorite patients while others sat and waited for me. The cats stretched and lazed about in the sun. The smaller animals I kept in their cages until I could take them personally to their respective patients.

"Damn," I said.

"What's the matter?" Trish asked.

"You let Esseltine escape just as I got a good price on a man-eating Bengal tiger. I was going to bring it along next weekend as a special present for him."

Trish let out the loudest laugh I'd heard in ages. "Oh, we have our own version of a Bengal Tiger. We let Bruno drive him home and get him set up. He told me he found every pothole in the road on the way to Esseltine's mansion. He even accidentally smacked the old man's head against the door jamb as he carried him through the front entrance."

"I'm surprised Bruno still has a job."

"I think even the old galoot knows better than to mess with Bruno although the hospital has received a request that a female nurse would be more welcome next time Esseltine needs to be transported. He demanded that we send a community nurse to care for him during the day. At our expense, of course."

"Of course. But I thought he was so serious he needed around-the-clock care."

"Leon, he has a few broken bones. Oh, and a broken personality. Despite the rumors that are getting about, he's as healthy as you and I. He won't be dying any time soon – unless it's murder. He just can't look after himself, so what he needs is someone to prepare his meals, bathe him, and generally push him about in his wheelchair."

My voice dripped with sarcasm. "Who won the lucky dip?"

"Trudy."

I rolled my eyes. Trudy was just the nicest person you could ever meet. Placid, caring, and sweet. Everyone loved Trudy. Nothing ruffled her equanimity. Nothing. Until she was seconded to look after Esseltine in his own home. In the space of a few days he managed to wipe the smile from her face, turn her personality from sunshine to thunder, and reduced her to tears. She also developed a mouth that cursed like the proverbial sailor. A week later she told Trish she would never return even if it meant she lost her job.

"I had a word to the Board to explain the situation and even those in Esseltine's pocket agreed the hospital cannot afford to kowtow to the miserable bastard's blackmail. They sent him a letter saying as much, not in those words, of course, suggesting he use some of his wealth to employ private nursing staff. Seems there were a lot of heated exchanges over the phone but Esseltine got the message. From now on, he's responsible for his own home care."

"We can all breathe easy again."

Now that he was gone, it was very easy to forget Ralph Esseltine moldering away in palatial splendor.

"It's not though," Bruno confided later when I congratulated him on his manhandling of the old miser. "Palatial splendor, I mean. I don't think I've ever been in a house that's more depressing. It's like it's taken on the personality of its owner. Dark and gloomy. The furniture is nothing to write home about. Sure, it's old, but it's not antique. More like something you'd get from a second-hand store. And everything's covered in dust except in the old dude's bedroom and his study. He doesn't use the other rooms any more. He's got that cook who's expected to double as a housekeeper comes in every day now and she does the best she can but it's not her really her department dusting and cleaning. Her name's Megan Hathaway. Old chook. Almost as old as Esseltine, so she's not exactly fast on her feet. Plus, the house is in need of urgent repair. Some of the rooms are so dilapidated that pigeons are roosting in holes in the ceiling. Still, he won't spend a dime to repair it. I wouldn't be surprised if the cook turns up one day to find him choked to death under vast layers of dust and mold."

"Sounds like karma to me," I said with some satisfaction.

"You can be hard sometimes, little dude."

I put the miserable misanthrope out of my mind. I had a life to live. It seems, however, the old bastard hadn't finished with me yet. Trish called me into the office one weekend after I'd distributed the animals among the patients out on the lawn and had taken some of the less rambunctious guinea pigs and cats inside to the serially bed-ridden. Things had settled back to normal six weeks after he'd gone home.

"It's nice around here again," I said as Trish motioned me to the well-padded leather armchair opposite her cluttered desk. She didn't appear to be her usual ebullient self. I refrained from banter because the situation seemed serious. I hoped my animals had not caused a problem. Trish must have read the distress on my face.

"No, Leon, it's nothing to do with your pets. Something more serious. I need a favor."

I owed Trish a lot so I was prepared to grant her anything. "If I can do it. What is it?"

"Megan, Mr. Esseltine's cook rang me yesterday."

It had to be serious because she called him Mr. Esseltine rather than just using his family name or any number of curse descriptors she had for patients like him.

I was wary. "Go on."

"He's taken a turn for the worse. It seems he's gone downhill since he went home. Megan does the best she can but she's not a nurse or a psychiatrist. He needs professional care. Like he would get here."

"If he wasn't such an asshole maybe he could come back."

Trish shuddered at the suggestion. "Megan asked if there was anything we could do to cheer him up."

I jumped up. "No, Trish. No. Not even for you."

"Please, Leon. Believe me, I respect how you feel. But he is a fellow human being—"

"Debatable," I groused.

"We owe him a duty of care."

"You might. I'm a vet. Remember. All I can do is give him a massive dose of ketamine."

The pleading went on for about half an hour during which I threw every objection I could think of into the mix while Trish cajoled, blackmailed, begged, promised, everything she could use from her armory. She wore me down.

"Okay. I'm doing what you ask with extreme reluctance. Please note the use of the word 'extreme.' I will not put up with any crap from him and, in particular, I will not allow him to abuse any animal I take to him. Is that understood?" Trish nodded. "And I will charge him a shitload of money for my services which I'll bill via the hospital."

Trish stood to shake hands, sealing the deal.

"It's on your head," I said.

"Megan's expecting you later this afternoon. Oh, by the way, Mr. Esseltine knows nothing about this."

I didn't like being bitchy but this reeked of a set-up. "Thanks for the ample notice."

I tried not to be grumpy while mingling with the patients, but the way I'd been shanghaied into the situation grated. I thought Trish was more of a friend than to drop me into an untenable situation.

"Hey, little buddy. Why the gloom?" Bruno put his arm around me comfortingly. After I explained the situation, he clasped me closer. "That's heavy shit, dude. I guess Trish thought you were the only person could handle it."

Whether Bruno believed that or said it merely to ease the tension in my mind, I wasn't sure, but I grabbed at straws. It helped calm me down so that I could plan my course of action without my personal animosity overwhelming me. "Thanks, Bruno. I owe you."

"I have heard that gay dudes give better head than chicks. Maybe I should test the theory," he laughed, swatting me on the butt.

"All gay propaganda," I replied because I knew he was teasing. "It's to get hot dudes like yourself interested enough to try at least once. We award trophies to those gay guys who blow the most straights. Extra points if you convert any of them permanently."

He gave me a thumbs up. "Thanks for the scoop, dude. I'll keep my pecker in my pants."

I was much too busy the rest of the day to give much thought to Esseltine. As he knew nothing of Megan's phone call, it would look as if I'd arrived uninvited. That was a catastrophe in the making. Why did I feel I was headed to my own execution later that afternoon as I packed up the animals to drive back to my kennels in the acreage behind my veterinary practice? Once they were settled, I couldn't put it off any longer. I would have taken Tynan as a companion but he'd already been on the receiving end of Esseltine's boot. Second choice was a friendly mutt, named Reggie.

Fortunately, the drive to the Esseltine residence was comparatively short along the expressway, otherwise I may have changed my mind and turned around to go back home. I pulled up at the impressive wrought iron gates to press the intercom. No one spoke but the gates swung open so there had to be video surveillance hidden somewhere in the stone wall or in a tree nearby. As the town was fairly crime-free it meant someone guarded their privacy jealously.

The pebbled driveway was not at all long and within seconds I pulled up at the front door. I saw the weather-worn wooden sign pointing the way to the

Tradesman's Entrance wondering whether I was expected to use that. They could expect all they want. Had I been delivering groceries, perhaps it would have been appropriate as it was obviously close to the kitchen, but I wasn't. I was delivering something more important: well-being.

Megan Hathaway scuttled around the corner of the mansion wiping her floury hands on her apron as I helped Reggie off the front seat of my van. Curious about his new surroundings, he wandered away to sniff the neglected flower beds – Esseltine was obviously too mean to pay for gardeners – and proclaim his territory by lifting his leg to spray against the stonework. Not sure that augured well for Esseltine's slippers.

"If you wouldn't mind coming this way, Mr. Paley," she instructed. She must have noticed my look of distaste at being forced to use the back entrance. "Just for today. Please. I mean no slight, but Mr. Esseltine doesn't know you're coming and I don't want to aggravate him by letting you in the front door. Not today."

This was not an auspicious beginning. Still, I smiled to assure her of my co-operation. She led me along the side of the house where the dilapidation was more obvious. The wood on the window sills was worn and flaking, the glass cracked and held together with black tape, the eaves rotting. Esseltine's next-of-kin would have an expensive task getting the old place up to scratch. Pity, it was a beautiful old relic.

The rear door had once been green as the faded paint bore witness. It now looked as if it had given up any attempt at cheerfulness although it opened into a warm, polished kitchen. It, at least, had been modernized although an old fuel stove had pride of place along one wall. It was kept in immaculate condition. I ran my hands along the enamel stove front and the jet black top. "This is beautiful, Mrs. Hathaway."

Her pleasure at my compliment showed in her eyes. "I give it as much attention as I can. My grandmother cooked on that stove. She worked for Mr. Esseltine's great grandparents. I used to sit in the corner as nan went about her business. It was always warm in here." She was woolgathering her memories for a few moments until we were interrupted by Reggie skittering through the back door looking for me.

"Sit down. I've made a sandwich in case you're hungry. I'll put the kettle on; make us a nice cuppa tea. Would your animal like something?"

"Reggie. His name is Reggie. Maybe a bowl of water."

He looked up at the mention of his name.

Megan addressed the dog. "I'd scratch behind your ears, love, but me hands are covered in flour." She turned to me. "Milk? Sugar? In your tea."

"Just as it pours, thanks, Mrs. Hathaway."

"Call me Megan, love. I haven't been Mrs. Hathaway since poor George dropped off the twig twenty years or more ago."

"And you should call me Leon."

She must have boiled the kettle in expectation of my arrival because in a matter of moments the water was whistling it was ready. Megan swirled a little around in the tea pot before adding leaf tea. I was surprised.

"Mr. Esseltine can't abide those awful bags. Thinks they're the devil's work. Can't say that I disagree with him but loose leaf is mucky and not as convenient. Still, he pays me well." Megan blushed as if she'd revealed State Secrets.

"My lips are sealed," I said, imitating a zip along my mouth.

She poured us both a mug of tea, no dainty porcelain china for us, topping hers with a copious amount of milk and three generous sugars. It must have been like drinking treacle. She'd prepared chicken sandwiches on crusty farm bread leavened with a thick layer of chutney. "Mm, these are really nice," I mumbled. I'd been living on the tasteless mass-produced white-bread sandwiches sold in convenience stores in a plastic box. Megan's were what real sandwiches should taste like. I picked out a piece of chicken to feed to Reggie who was sitting patiently on the stone floor, thumping his tail in an attempt to attract my attention. One piece, though, was never going to be enough. As I chomped my way through the remainder, sharing every now and then with the ever patient Reggie, Megan explained her dilemma.

"I've worked for the Esseltines all me life," she said after taking a giant sip of tea to screw up her courage. "I've never gone against me instructions before but I can't bear to see him like this."

"Like what?" I enquired.

Megan became teary. "Like he's given up all hope. Like he wants to die."

"Is there anything wrong with him? Medically, I mean?"

"Just old age. He's in his eighties now so, of course, things are starting to slow down. But his mind is as sharp as a tack."

"And his temper," I added, none too kindly.

She nodded. "He's always had that."

Megan had a plan of sorts – not a very good one – but I'd have to go along with it as I couldn't think of anything better. Esseltine usually had his afternoon tea on the back terrace. It was shady and paved evenly enough for his wheelchair to which he now seemed permanently confined. "He has a few dried biscuits and his pot of tea. He sits staring out at the view for about an hour before he rings to be brought back inside."

Just then, a bell tinkled. I looked up to see a row of them labeled with the section of the house that required service. It was the Study. Megan immediately set up a tray with a plate of desiccated biscuits that looked as appetizing as a mouthful of Sahara sand, and a pot of leaf tea. The service all appeared to be of the finest china, probably worth more than my entire veterinary practice was worth.

"He'll be a little while as he has to make his way from up there." She pointed at the ceiling. "He has one of those thingamabobs that moves his wheelchair down the stairs."

"An Inclinator."

"Could be. This new electronic age is not meant for someone as old as me."

She must have been just a few years younger than Esseltine but she looked life-weary, her face creviced with wrinkles. She ran her hand through her straggly red hair that was in need of a touch-up as the gray was beginning to show, like thin streaks of flour in the strands. "Here, let me help you," I said.

"No. Not yet. Your sudden appearance would give him a heart attack. Let him have his first cuppa. That usually puts him in a mellow mood. Then I'll take you through as if you've just turned up."

"What exactly is my excuse for being here?"

She picked up the tray to make her way to the stairs. "I'm sure you'll think of something. You're a bright young man."

Megan's plan was looking less like a strategy and more and more like a disaster waiting to happen. What on earth could I come up with as an excuse for visiting the Esseltine mansion, something I would normally never consider even with a gun shoved against my temple? I was none the wiser when Megan returned.

"How is he today?" I asked.

"Melancholy," she smiled.

"And that's good?"

"Better than angry."

"Is he angry with you very often?"

"Not with me, no. Angry at the world. Angry with himself. I think he regrets casting out his daughter. Melissa."

"She married someone he didn't approve of, didn't she?"

"Not so much that he didn't approve of. More that her boyfriend wasn't the suitor he chose for her himself. He hoped the marriage would be a disaster and she'd come back to him chastised, tail between her legs. Then he'd be ever so supportive, have the marriage annulled, and then marry her off to his choice which would have consolidated his business dealings."

I was horrified. "He wanted his own daughter to marry for business rather than for love? In this day and age?"

She shrugged. "It was no more than he did for his own parents. It was expected. But she was wild. She had her own mind. In the end, she chose love over family."

"Did it make her happy?"

"She wrote to me every now and then. Like when she had Rohan, her son. I thought that may have been the thing that healed the rift between father and daughter. But, no. He wouldn't even look at the photographs."

"What happened to her?"

Megan's sharp intake of breath sounded like an attempt to stifle a sob. "Melissa died in childbirth. Somehow the delivery went terribly wrong. She lost a lot of blood. The baby, a little sister for Rohan, was stillborn and Melissa died the following day. Of complications I think the verdict was. Her husband wrote to me with the news. A few days later he put a pistol in his mouth and…" She was unable to go on.

I wrapped my arms around her as she sobbed silently into my shirt. After a few moments, she wiped her eyes on her apron. "Look at the time. We'd better get you out on the terrace otherwise he'll be calling to be taken back inside."

She led me from the kitchen through the darkened house, brisk enough that I scarcely had time to register anything, until she paused at the bay window. Esseltine had his back to us but the stoop of his shoulders and the way his head sagged was enough to reveal that here was a man who had given up. Megan straightened her apron, pushed stray hairs behind her ears, took a deep breath and then opened the double glass doors to step out onto the terrace. I followed, none too sure this was going to have the desired effect.

"Look who just popped in," Megan said brightly as we approached, Esseltine attempting a half-turn to see.

It wasn't until I stood in front of him that it seemed to register. "You," he spat. "Show him the door, Mrs. Hathaway."

She fussed over him, patting and prodding him to make him more comfortable, and to deflect his anger.

"Now, that's no way to treat someone who's come all this way to see us, is it, Mr. Esseltine?"

He wasn't about to be appeased. "What do you want?" he snapped.

My mind went into overdrive until I came up with the only plausible excuse for being there. I hated doing it. "I came to apologize for Tynan."

"Who the hell is Tynan? And why can't he do his own apologizing?"

"Tynan is a dog. I'm afraid his English is lacking and can't beg your forgiveness himself."

Esseltine seemed to take my feeble attempt at humor as sarcasm. "Is that the mutt who pissed in my slippers?"

Megan was biting her lower lip. Obviously this meeting was not going well. "Righto," she said as breezily as she could muster, "I'll leave you two to get better acquainted."

"You'll do no such thing. Mrs. Hathaway, I have nothing further to discuss with this person. Please remove him from my house."

She pretended she didn't hear him as she made her way back inside, I suspect very grateful to escape.

"Mind if I sit down?" I asked. It never hurt to be polite.

"Yes. Piss off. I don't want you or your belated apology."

None the less, I pulled out the chair opposite and sat down.

"Are you deaf as well as stupid?" he snapped.

I smiled although it was the sort of smile a shark might make. "Pardon?"

He didn't find it amusing. "What's your name?"

"Leon Paley." I spelt out my family name. "Just so you get it right when you send off a letter to your cronies about having me dismissed."

His face lit up with recognition. "You're Joel Paley's son. I should have known the twig wouldn't fall far from the tree. A more useless man I never met."

I was up out of my seat, my temper ready to give him both barrels. "You can say—" That was the moment Reggie decided to catapult around the side of the house in pursuit of a few stray pigeons. Esseltine looked in horror from my apoplectic red face to my clenched fists to the dog, visions of Tynan's disgrace obviously fresh in his mind. Reggie stopped in mid chase when he saw me. The pigeons had already flown out of reach so the happy dog shot over toward me and what he obviously saw as his new best friend. Reggie had only one speed when it came to humans: faster than a speeding bullet. Esseltine cowered at the approach, attempting to wheel away. Reggie yapped, thinking the old man was playing some sort of a game. The more

Reggie snapped at Esseltine's heels and barked playfully, the more concerned the old man appeared, backing away as if being attacked by some sort of monster.

Esseltine kicked out at Reggie which just made the dog mad. When Reggie began to growl, I knew things were getting out of hand. Unfortunately, the more I called for Reggie to heel, the more it just added to the cacophony of noise. Megan had come to the door and watched in horror as Esseltine's foot finally connected with Reggie, knocking him flying against the table with a startled yelp. That in turn knocked the china sideways. I watched paralyzed, unable to prevent the unfolding catastrophe as the crockery fell to the stone in seemingly slow motion, shattering into a thousand pieces. Esseltine roared, kicking out wildly in frustration, connecting again with Reggie who howled in pain.

I lost it. I had my hand around Esseltine's throat, choking the living daylights out of him as Megan hurried toward me, a look of horror on her face. Gritting my teeth, I snarled in Esseltine's face covering him with spit, "You will never disrespect my father's name ever in future. And you not kick my dogs, no matter what their behavior. Do you hear me?"

Esseltine was in no position to answer as I'd cut off his breath and he was turning purple in the face. Megan laid her hand on my back. "No, Mr. Paley. This is not the way."

I released Esseltine's throat, and he gasped for breath. "You are one miserable old bastard," I snapped, then I picked up a very subdued Reggie, cradling him in my arms, talking soothingly as I turned and fled to my van. "I'll have the police on to you," Esseltine shouted.

Reggie looked at me with sad eyes. "No, baby," I soothed. "It wasn't your fault." I knew it was mine.

Back home, I examined Reggie for injury but found no broken bones. He wasn't limping, in fact, he seemed to have forgotten the incident and was keen to get outside and play. I released him, wondering whether I had over-reacted. It was unlike me to lose my temper. I had never threatened anyone before in my life. Yes, there were extenuating circumstances, Esseltine had insulted my father and had kicked my dog – twice – but to strangle the life out of a sick old man…

I went to my office and typed out my resignation from the hospital, effective immediately. I clicked Send. Even though I donated my services, it was the right thing to do. That way Esseltine would have no comeback at Trish. I hoped Megan would be all right up at the mansion. It had been all her idea but I didn't want her to suffer. Her concern was admirable; my execution of it was the problem. I wondered whether I would have a veterinarian practice by the end of the week. Esseltine owned the building and the land. I was on a week-to-week lease because I'd never thought to renegotiate. Too late now.

Knowing the shit would hit the fan shortly, expecting a visit from the police, I packed an overnight bag and turned the taps on for a nice hot bath. I scattered a handful of bath salts – lavender and some other herb I'd never heard of – into the water, tested it with my fingers, added a little cold water and then slid into its welcoming warmth. I relaxed, leaning back against the cold enamel, finally putting my agitation to rest. I wondered if the attack on Esseltine was enough to have the cops put Reggie to sleep. I'd have to hide him with a friend for a few days, tell the authorities he was so traumatized he'd run away.

I hopped out of the bath and toweled myself dry, dressing in a clean outfit to wait. I was surprised there were no messages on my voicemail or any record of missed calls. It was obviously the calm before the storm. When nothing else happened in the next hour, I made myself a meal although it tasted like sawdust and I couldn't finish it. I scraped it into the hen house trough where appetites were not so discerning.

If the police insisted on keeping me in the cells I would need an assistant to care for the sick and injured animals as well as the menagerie I kept for myself. I sighed. Nothing had gone right since I'd met Esseltine.

At midnight, I decided it was time to go to bed. No phone calls, no cops, but I couldn't sleep, tossing about in the bed, my mind creating so many different scenarios – none of them good – for what would happen the next day. Exhaustion finally overtook me in the early hours of the morning.

The unexpected sound of my cell phone had me gasping for breath as I sat up in my bed. It was Patti Page warbling 'How much is that Doggie in the Window?' – the ring tone I used for the hospital. Still groggy from lack of sleep, I sounded like a drunken chipmunk. "Hello?"

The voice on the other end was so cheerful it gave me a headache. "Way to go, dude. I hear you almost throttled the old bastard to death in his wheelchair. You, man, are my new hero."

"What do you want, Bruno?" I croaked.

"To worship at your feet, little dude. But what I'm ringing about is a message from the boss herself."

I groaned.

"She wants your ass in here like an hour ago. I've never seen her like this. I tried to slip a Valium in her coffee but she was wise to me. I gotta say, man, we all support you though. If you get the electric chair, I'll even let you blow me so you go to meet your maker with a smile on your face."

I had a smile now for the first time since the 'incident.'

"Don't tempt me, Bruno. I might actually kill him next time."

"My ass is not too high a price to pay to witness that."

"Tell Trish I'll be there in an hour."

"Hey, Leon?" Bruno rarely used my name. "Hang in there. It'll be all right."

"Thanks, Bruno." I wished I had his confidence.

I skipped the shower because I had to feed the animals and that took most of my time. I hoped I covered the slight stink of my armpits with a spray of cologne on my shirt. Whether I'd be able to return to the sick and maimed in my vet hospital all depended on Esseltine. Although I felt sorry enough for myself – it had taken a while but the townsfolk had finally grown to accept me – it was the animals and the pet owners who concerned me more. They would have to go to the next town, about eight kilometers away, in future for pet care once I was closed down.

All the way to Callicoma Hospital, I wracked my brain to figure out a way to make things right. Impossible. I had almost killed old Esseltine. After he'd already lost a pair of slippers to Tynan. Now he'd lost an expensive set of china. It was beyond my means to pay for it. I expected the worst.

I found a spot in the hospital car park. With leaden feet I made my way through the corridors, passing various wards with names of local benefactors, until I reached the office marked Patricia Nolan Administrator. I tapped lightly. "Enter," she called. I went into the room, unsurprised that Dave Chason was seated opposite her.

"I'll come back," I said, backing toward the door.

"No, come in, Leon. Dave is here to see you."

That was the last thing I wanted to hear. Chason was the local cop. There was no escape. I shook his hand in greeting. Trish nodded to the spare chair. I slumped, unable to look at either of them.

Trish started the meeting. "This is what I think of your resignation." She picked up a print-out and tore it in half before crumpling it to toss in the bin.

"It's a lovely gesture, Trish, but that was a blank piece of paper. Besides, the Board would have your guts for garters."

Trish shrugged. "The printer's on the blink. It was a symbolic gesture."

"I appreciate it." I turned to Chason. "You here to arrest me?"

He shifted uncomfortably in his chair. "That's the thing, Leon. He's not going to press charges even though his doctor said he had some pretty nasty bruises to the throat where you tried to strangle him."

I couldn't relax just yet. "But?"

"It seems attempted murder is just fine by Mr. Esseltine, but when it comes to a pair of slippers, and fine china, it's another matter altogether." He handed me an invoice. "That's the cost of what you and your dogs destroyed."

I blanched at the figure at the bottom of the page. "My god. The slippers cost more than I earn in a month."

"Unless you want to have a heart conniption, don't look at the cost of the china," Trish warned.

Too late, I'd already seen it. I put my hands out to Chason. "Cuff me now. I don't have that sort of money."

Chason interrupted my performance. "Hold your horses, Leon. Mr. Esseltine is willing to do a deal."

I didn't like the sound of that. "What, I have to donate a kidney, a heart, a lung, to keep the old bastard alive?"

"See, it's an attitude like that gets you into trouble," Chason said. "He's doing you a favor, Leon."

I snapped. "Cut the crap, Chason. Ralph Esseltine doesn't do favors, he does humiliation."

"You know he's right, Dave," Trish added on my behalf.

"Whatever," he shrugged.

"So what does he want?" I was impatient to get this over with and get on with what was left of my life.

Chason cleared his throat, meaning this was all official now. "Mr. Esseltine knows you are unlikely to have the ready money to replace his hand-crafted slippers and his antique bone china so has generously—"

I guffawed.

"—generously allowed you the opportunity to work it off. Four evenings a week you will be expected at his residence to attend to any chores he deems necessary."

I dug my heels in. "I will not wipe the old bastard's ass."

Trish laughed. "I doubt he'd trust you to do that, Leon."

Chason was eager to continue. "If you complete said tasks to his satisfaction, he will waive any claims he has against you. A contract will be drawn up and signed by you and Mr. Esseltine to make the entire matter legal. What do you say?"

There was a major item missing from what I'd been told. "Exactly how long is this contract to last?"

"One year," Chason said.

I was speechless. Well, almost. "A year? What about my social life?"

"What social life? You don't have one," Trish said. "Take the deal, Leon. You can go without what you haven't had for ages for another year. I don't want to lose the best thing that's happened to the hospital since I started work here."

"You mean he hasn't made it a condition that I stop bringing the pets to the hospital?"

"There's no stipulation about cats, dogs, mice, gerbils, rattlesnakes or orca whales," Chason said.

I sighed. "But, a year."

Chason added cheerfully, "We're taking bets you won't last more than a week or two but that gives you time to find a locum to look after your vet practice while you're inside playing bitch to Big Bad Brad or whatever his name will be."

I couldn't see any way out of it. "Please inform Mr. Esseltine that I agree to his terms and to draw up the contract."

I shook hands with Chason, who seemed relieved, and shook my head at Trish who looked as if she agreed that this was not a good idea. What choice did I have?

I was very chastened by the time I returned home and only the patients in my waiting room took my mind off my rapidly unraveling life. I could do this provided I kept focused. Trish was right, I had no social life to speak off. I'd had a few furtive experiences since I'd arrived in Callicoma three years before but nothing memorable and nothing lasting. I drove into the city if I needed relief, usually more than happy to return home from the dispiriting lovemaking of a one-night stand to my true love: caring for animals. No man had captured my heart like Tynan, or Reggie, or any of the others since Paul and I split up.

He didn't like pets. Potted plants were the limit of his appreciation of other species and those he treated in such a cavalier fashion they usually died of neglect. The only thing he appreciated more than himself was a stiff dick, and toward the end of our relationship it was anyone else's dick but mine. Familiarity had bred boredom and he soon moved on to others until I called a halt to the whole forlorn experience, escaping the city to the large regional town of Callicoma where I buried my hurt and disgust in my work.

Another year of that sort of social life I could well do without.

Mid-afternoon I received a phone call from the secretary at Ryan, Fielding & Colbert asking me to attend later that afternoon. There was an implied 'or else' in her voice when I began prevaricating. "Mr.

Fielding expects you at 5.30. Please be on time. Time is money, Mr. Paley." She hung up on me before I could respond. I would make the effort. I didn't want to get off to a bad start.

As it was, 5.30 came and went as I sat in the waiting area at the lawyer's office. When 6PM came and went as well, I'd had enough. I went to the receptionist whose voice sounded like the woman I'd spoken with earlier. I couldn't resist it. "I was told to be here at 5.30. It is now 6PM. As you know, time is money. Please inform Mr. Fielding I have better things to do with my life than wait on him when he doesn't have the courtesy of a cane toad. He could have, at least, informed me he was going to be late. Good evening."

She looked abashed that anyone would take that attitude with her but before she could respond the door opened and a distinguished middle-aged gent strode through the door. He was all smiles, thrusting out his hand in greeting. "You must be Mr. Paley. My sincere apologies for keeping you waiting. I've just been with Mr. Esseltine going over last-minute fine tuning of your contract. Please come inside. Two coffees, please, Miss Pinkerton."

I was ushered into an office so palatial it would have been at home in *Luxurious Law Firms* magazine – if there were one. Instead of sitting behind his beautiful wooden desk that was almost as big as a yacht and was the hue of a classic claret, he steered me to a comfortable leather couch where he spread a few sheets of paper on the glass and chrome coffee table.

"It's all very straightforward, Mr. Paley, but it's my duty to go through it with you so you thoroughly understand what it is your signing."

"Enlighten me." I couldn't help my sarcasm.

Miss Pinkerton supplied us with a rather superior coffee, cream, sugar, and a plate of imported biscuits that might have come from the Queen's own bakery. That mellowed me a little although as Mr. Fielding read out each paragraph of the Esseltine contract my blood threatened to reach boiling point. As he explained paragraph eleven, I interrupted. "I was under the belief that slavery had been abolished."

Fielding had the good graces to smile at my little joke. "Under the circumstances, I believe Mr. Esseltine's offer is more than generous. Particularly, as you attempted to choke him to death."

"All right, I get the point. Where do I sign?"

"I don't think you understand the importance of fully reading a contract."

"I understand only too well. What choice do I have but to sign?"

He coughed in embarrassment. "None."

"So why subject me to this tedious legal gobbledygook which is threatening to explode my brain with boredom when I will be obliged to put my signature at the bottom no matter what it says."

"You're very forthright, Mr. Paley."

"I have a low threshold for bullshit," I replied. "Tell me, is there anything in the contract of which I should be wary?"

"Nothing at all."

"All right then. I have one condition of my own."

"I don't think—"

"I don't really care what you think one way or the other, Mr. Fielding. I will only sign the document provided a paragraph of my own is inserted stating that Mr. Esseltine will not attempt to remove me from my premises unless I do something illegal and that he will not raise my rent above fluctuations in the real estate market."

"That seems fair." Fielding buzzed the receptionist and asked her to get Mr. Esseltine on the phone. In less than five minutes, Esseltine had agreed to my demand. Fielding had the new paragraph added to the contract and I signed it. My first meeting with Esseltine, as his personal slave, was the following evening.

It was best to get it out of the way sooner rather than later. If I'd had longer to think about it I may have reneged on the deal even though Fielding informed me the penalty was severe. Esseltine would not only apply to the court for reparation for the damage I had caused but would also charge me with assault. It would not look good that a strong, healthy young man had attempted to throttle a wheelchair-bound man in his eighties, even though Fielding smiled kindly and whispered, "You merely did what I and so many in the town have never had the courage to do ourselves. You've gained quite a reputation for yourself, young man."

Right on time, I presented myself at the front door of the mansion. Mrs. Hathaway answered. She began to stutter an apology for luring me into trouble but I dismissed it, "It was all my own fault. He riled me but I should have kept my temper."

"He's waiting for you in his study. I'll show you the way."

The mansion was gloomy as if it was exhausted from too much past, from too many unhappy memories, ghosts of joyless decades. It made me shiver even though the corridors were warm. Mrs. Hathaway, as she would be from now on as I was merely another member of staff, albeit unpaid, led me upstairs and along yet another corridor until she stopped in front of a door and knocked. "Enter," Esseltine called. Mrs.

Hathaway opened the door and announced, without entering, "Mr. Paley is here, sir."

"Ah, I do appreciate punctuality. Come in Mr. Paley. That will be all Mrs. Hathaway."

I entered the room and the door closed behind me. "Please take a seat. I'll be with you in a moment." I watched as he perused the papers on his desk through a large magnifying glass. The room was illuminated by a single modern lamp that was adjusted over his desk, heavy curtains pulled shut against the fading sunshine outside. When he was satisfied with the papers he was examining, he handed a set to me. "Here is your copy of the contract, Mr. Paley. I assume that Mr. Fielding explained it all to you."

I leaned over to take the sheets, folding them away in my coat pocket. "Until it did my head in and then I told him I didn't want to hear any more."

"One should always read the fine print, Mr. Paley."

"I'm sure one should but when one has the choice of a prison term or signing one's life away it's best the nasties lurking in the fine print come as a pleasant surprise."

"I can assure you there are no nasty surprises, Mr. Paley."

"Then let's cut the crap and get down to the nuts and bolts. Why am I here?"

"To pay off your debts to me, of course."

"Okay, so how many kilos of humiliation would you like? How much abject groveling? How much petty genuflecting to your money and prestige is required? Let's get over this civil bullshit we're both pretending and get right down to what you really want which is to hang me out to dry in front of the entire population of Callicoma as a warning to anyone else who crosses you."

He laughed. Actually laughed. "I knew I did the right thing in bringing you here, Mr. Paley. Let me explain something to you. You intrigue me. That's not something I can say of many people I've met." I think my look of surprise said it all. "However, we'll leave that discussion for another day. You are here to entertain me, Mr. Paley. My eyesight is not what it once was so your first task will be to read to me."

I had visions of reading contracts and stock reports and other items that were dry as dust. Instead, Esseltine handed me a leather-bound edition. "We'll start with that. I do hope you read well, Mr. Paley."

If it's something I loved almost as much as animals, it was reading aloud. I was notorious at school for being the first to volunteer. Whether the old grouch would be sufficiently impressed, it was impossible to say. If all I had to do for the next year was read aloud, my punishment would be a breeze.

I turned to the spine. I was to read Charles Dickens. I kept my smile to myself thinking there could be no more Dickensian character than Esseltine himself. The surprise was that he had chosen the author's last completed story, *Our Mutual Friend.* I was unfamiliar with the novel so it was an added treat to read it aloud. Esseltine sat back in his seat, his hands steepled on the desk, his eyes closed.

That was all very well for him and his fading eyesight but I was seated in shadow, the illumination from his lamp suitable only if I leaned onto his desk. Perhaps it was a test.

I stood and walked to the curtains. "Please tell me now if you are a vampire, Mr. Esseltine, although I would be less than heartbroken to reduce you to dust by exposing you to the sun's rays, but I'm afraid I am unable to read in darkness." I swept the curtains aside to allow the sunlight to flood the room. The rays revealed a veritable flood of dust mites which caught in my nostrils making me sneeze. Fresh air was the answer but the window wouldn't budge until I pulled with all my strength and it finally gave way with the sort of screech I'd expect from a wounded animal. I dusted my hands on my trousers before reclaiming my seat and pick up the novel. It was only then I noticed Esseltine's mouth agape.

"Perhaps you expected I had extraordinary vision, Mr. Esseltine. Well, let me disabuse you of the idea that I have superpowers. I am but a humble veterinarian and regardless of the myths about carrots and rabbits, I have ordinary vision." I hoped my sarcasm got through.

"You are very impertinent, Mr. Paley." He chuckled then. "A vampire. Indeed."

I opened at the first page and began to read. "In these times of ours, though concerning the exact year there is no need to be precise, a boat of dirty and disreputable appearance, with two figures in it, floated on the Thames, between Southwark Bridge, which is of iron, and London Bridge which is of stone, as an autumn evening was closing in…"

As I continued the story which seemed to be preoccupied with money and human values, arranged marriages, and inheritance, I began to wonder at Esseltine's choice of material. I also wondered whether my voice had put him to sleep as he had his eyes closed but, as if to assure me of his attention, he would sometimes ask me to repeat a passage or else mutter his approval at a particularly apposite turn of phrase. Occasionally, as I read, my confidence increasing with every page, I wondered whether I had perhaps become trapped in a time warp and I was a character in a novel that Dickens forgot to write and that Esseltine was a male incarnation of someone like Miss Haversham.

Time passed quickly until my reading was abruptly and rudely interrupted by the grumbling of my stomach. Esseltine opened his eyes and allowed me to finish the sentence before he looked at his watch. "You read very well, Mr. Paley. I'm impressed. But I have kept you, and your stomach reminded me that you have other duties. I asked Mrs. Hathaway to prepare a light supper for you. You will find her in the kitchen. Until next time." I was dismissed.

I returned the novel, open at the page I'd reached, to Esseltine and he inserted a leather book mark before placing it on the edge of his desk where I would find it on my next visit.

Downstairs in the kitchen, Mrs. Hathaway awaited me with some trepidation. When I appeared, she made quite a fuss over me as if she expected that I had murdered and mutilated her employer. A wedge of steaming home-made meat pie, crust as crisp as an autumn morning, along with a tomato and a little salad awaited me. I'd forgotten I hadn't eaten since breakfast while engrossed in reading to Esseltine.

"How was it?" she asked. I could call her Megan now that we weren't mixing in any official capacity.

I had to think about her question for a while and only then admitted, very reluctantly, that I had quite enjoyed myself. Perhaps I had misjudged the man but then I thought of all the terrible things he'd done in his life and had to rethink my position. My mind argued with itself attempting to persuade me that people are not all bad or all good. I settled on that premise because it enabled me to be civil to the old man, otherwise my bitterness might spill over into my 'community' service.

As no one but the lawyer and those folk at the mansion itself knew I'd begun my servitude, there were no phone calls asking for a rundown. I was grateful and, two afternoons later, arrived at Esseltine's front door on the dot. I normally spent two hours reading and finishing off a delicious supper which was always laid on for me. By the second week, my visits still secret outside those in the know, I actually began to look forward to the task, especially when Esseltine sighed after a particularly impressive section and said, "Dickens really knew how to paint a picture with words."

I agreed with him. At the end of that session he actually asked my opinion of various passages and what I thought of them and what they said about Dickens the man. He listened attentively to my opinions, interrupting only to get me to clarify something or other, waiting until I'd finished at which time he was free with his point of view. Sometimes we disagreed, oft times we agreed. I believed we were both stimulated by the friendly discussion of ideas.

Two weeks after I'd begun my visits, Trish called me into her office on the Sunday to enquire when I was to begin my contracted hours with Esseltine. She was surprised when I told her I already had.

"Go on. Spill," she instructed. "How long do you think it will be before you batter him to death with his own meanness?"

"Hard as it is for me to say this, I'm enjoying my time with Ralph Esseltine."

I thought her coffee would shoot out her nose she was so surprised. "Pardon me?"

"He's got me reading Dickens to him for about ninety minutes, then we have a short discussion after which I head to the kitchen for a light supper with Megan Hathaway. It's all rather jolly."

"Tell me you just made that up."

"It's true."

"Who are you and what have you done with Leon Paley?" she asked.

A number of people, including Bruno, asked the same question once they discovered what I'd been up to for the previous two weeks. It became tiresome very quickly and I wished I'd kept my mouth shut. I was made to feel like a traitor. I hadn't changed my mind about Esseltine's behavior or his stingy attitude to money, but I had to give credit where it was due; he was rather civilized when it came to great literature. He'd even suggested the second book could be my choice as long as it wasn't an airport time-filler and he'd rather I didn't choose Stephen King because his novels rather scared the bejesus out of him. I still hadn't decided between E.M. Forster and something more recent.

By the end of the first month people had stopped badgering me about Esseltine and found other things to discuss, although both Bruno and Trish still looked at me strangely, as if I'd grown an extra head. It was as if we inhabited parallel universes.

Truth is I began to miss my visits to the mansion on the days I didn't have to turn up. Megan commented on how my presence cheered the old man, how she'd never seen him so chipper. She believed I was a good influence on him, letting slip that Esseltine's moods darkened and he fretted on the days I had free. As a result I spent more time on the weekends at the mansion after I'd finished at the hospital. On those occasions, I read to him on the terrace in the afternoon sunshine although we were mostly shaded by the house.

It was on one such occasion that I had an idea that might help him overcome his obvious loneliness. It was a big chance to take considering the strides we'd made. I couldn't call our relationship close and we certainly would never be friends but the feeling of animosity was gone. I got the impression he was as pleased to see me as I was to be there. We were well into Forster's *A Room with a View* after he'd ridiculed my choice of author as 'that pacifist fag' although he was enchanted by the story now. In fact, Esseltine enjoyed it so much I bought him a copy of the movie on DVD. Alas, I hadn't anticipated that his home would be devoid of such twentieth century marvels as a TV and a DVD player.

"For Pete's sake, Mr. Esseltine," I complained when I discovered my gift was useless, "I know you don't like spending any of your hard-earned cash but a flat screen and a DVD player are not going to bankrupt you. We could have watched the movie together and discussed how it differed from the novel."

About a week later, Megan Hathaway met me at the door in an agitated state. "You won't believe what he's gone and done."

My heart sank for a moment. "Has he injured himself?" My opinion of Esseltine as a thoroughly despicable human being had not changed but I didn't wish him harm.

"Worse than that."

"He's dead?"

"Don't be silly, the man's as strong as an ox. No, he spent some money. I couldn't believe my eyes. Come and I'll show you."

I was intrigued. Of course, Esseltine spent money on food and utilities and Megan's meager wages so I realized the consternation was over something that he would consider a luxury. What struck me most was that I was shown into the downstairs living room. I'd peeked into it once but got such an attack of the sneezes from the accumulation of dust that the mere thought of entering the room again almost brought on an attack of asthma. I needn't have worried as the room had been dusted and cleaned. The furniture had been rearranged and the plush leather lounge now took pride of place opposite the latest model 42-inch plasma screen and a top-of-the range Blu-ray player.

I gaped at the changes, so surprised I failed to notice Esseltine in his wheelchair patiently awaiting my arrival. "Well, what do you think?" he asked.

I didn't know what to say and told him honestly. That satisfied him.

"I'd hate to think I was predictable," he muttered. "Well, don't just stand there. I had the people at the showroom set it up because I couldn't make head or tail of the instructions. The salesman said they were in English but it's not any sort of English that I know. Stop looking so surprised and put the bloody thing in the player and let's get on with it. You haven't got all night and I know there'll be hell to pay if I keep you one second longer than you have to be here."

I took the disc from the plastic case and went to insert it in the player. "Mr. Esseltine, strange as it may sound, I've come to like the evenings I spend here and you will never hear a complaint from me should we forget the time because we're enjoying each other's company."

He coughed and huffed as if too embarrassed to respond. He covered it by bellowing for Mrs. Hathaway. She scuttled to the door. "Yes, sir?"

"Could you manage a pot of tea…or, Mr. Paley, would you prefer coffee?"

"Tea is fine, especially the way Mrs. Hathaway brews it," I replied.

"A pot of tea and a few biscuits," he continued.

I had visions of those crackers he devoured that were as dried up as his shriveled skin. "Did you order those Jaffa Orange Cake biscuits I asked you about?"

"I did, sir."

"Then bring a packet. No, bring two packets. And I'd like you to join us for the film, Mrs. Hathaway."

She was so startled by the invitation I wondered whether she might head straight to the phone and ring to have Esseltine carted away for psychiatric examination. But she brought a plate of chocolate biscuits which Esseltine pounced on as soon as she placed them on the coffee table. "I used to love these as a child but my father thought they were much too indulgent. I used to save my pocket money to buy a packet and smuggle it into my bedroom. I'd forgotten all about them. I have no idea what triggered the memory," he said as he ate the biscuit with obvious relish.

Mrs. Hathaway poured us all a mug of tea. I flinched when I saw that Esseltine no longer drank from fine china but from a mug with SpongeBob SquarePants on the side. It was the most incongruous sight of all. I turned off all the lights except for a standard lamp beside the flat screen, took my place on the lounge next to Mrs. Hathaway who was much too nervous to sit still, while Esseltine sat in his wheelchair to one side. I took a biscuit, moved my mug of hot tea within easy reach, and pressed play on the remote control. I'd seen the Merchant-Ivory film before so it was a wonder watching Megan and Esseltine's reaction. Megan was enthralled although I knew she occasionally went to the cinema with one or two of her female friends, but Esseltine was like a young kid who'd been taken to the movies for the first time. He kept stuffing his face with biscuits, washing them down with sips of tea.

The end came much too soon for all of us. Mrs. Hathaway hurried off to the kitchen while Esseltine asked about some of the actors in the film. I did my best to enlighten him before we turned our attention to how successfully the novel had been adapted to the screen. We were still discussing it an hour later after we'd both eaten our supper in the living room; plates perched on our knees, Mrs. Hathaway long since gone home for the night.

Now, days later, I was about to risk throwing the whole enterprise down the toilet if my plan didn't work. I was counting on Esseltine being concerned that I hadn't arrived on time as usual and that he'd be relieved when I did show up. He was waiting for me on the terrace seemingly spooked at my tardiness. I apologized profusely saying I'd been unavoidably detained at the hospital and that I'd got there as fast as possible, so fast, in fact, I hadn't had a chance to offload my cargo of animals at home before I arrived.

"I just called in to tell you I'll be about an hour once I drive back to my surgery and feed and pen the animals," I explained patiently. "Of course, I'll make up for my lateness by staying later."

Esseltine was irritable. "The sun will be gone by the time you return. We'll have to go inside and I much prefer it out here. This is most inconvenient. Can't you just leave the stupid creatures in the back of your van until we finish?"

I felt like smacking him. He had no consideration for anyone or anything other than himself. But I held my tongue: I didn't need another assault charge. "It's far too hot to leave them in there for any length of time. They fret. Plus they're all in cages so they need to stretch their muscles before they get cramps." I was laying it on thick for his benefit.

"Isn't there something you can do to save you having to go home?" He was so miserable I sprang my trap.

"Well, you have lovely grounds here, if I could let them roam free for exercise, then I wouldn't have to make the journey home at the moment. I could stay and read to you."

I saw the battle raging within him written large on his face. Pleasure of being read to versus wild animals charging about his property. He exhaled loudly. "They're not vicious, are they? They won't attack me?"

"All my animals are well-trained and well-behaved."

"Still, I've been attacked twice by these so-called trained creatures," he complained.

"In all fairness you did kick them on both occasions."

"Animals don't like me," he moaned. "They never have."

"It's all in the way you handle them."

He huffed impatiently. "Go ahead. Release your bloody wild animals. Just keep them away from me. Understood?"

"Understood," I said.

Of course, I had already taken most of the animals home, surfeited from the petting at the hospital. I had a few of the larger dogs who liked to run riot in large properties but I knew they would keep themselves occupied chasing the colored balls I threw to the farthest ends of the gardens after I released them from their dog boxes. They would leave Esseltine well alone. Lastly, I cradled the cutest Labrador puppy and walked back to the terrace where Esseltine waited.

"I thought I told you—"

"This is Max," I interrupted. "He's very shy around strangers. He's just a few months old. He'll be no bother. I can hold him as I read to you. He's much too young and timid to attack you."

Esseltine didn't look convinced. "All right, if you must." Max looked at him with those big brown eyes. I wondered how he could resist.

Picking up the new book, Esseltine's choice was Siegfried Sassoon's *Memoirs of a Fox-Hunting Man* which struck me as the incredibly homoerotic memoirs of a gay youth. I mentioned it to him in passing but his nostrils flared and his eyes narrowed until I shut up and just went on with reading. As much as I abhorred fox hunting and any sort of blood sports, I found the book compelling. I was glad Esseltine had chosen it.

I moved my chair closer to him as I turned to the page at which we'd stopped the previous visit. I'd noticed that Esseltine was having difficulty hearing me sometimes. I wondered if he was going deaf. I didn't dare broach the subject.

I made sure the larger dogs were still tearing about at the bottom of the garden before I began reading aloud. Max shifted on my lap from time to time and I noticed Esseltine kept a wary eye on him in case he attacked. The sound of my voice must have made Max tired because he yawned, the sight of his teeth and long wet pink tongue causing Esseltine to flinch. At his most vicious, the worst Max could do was lick him to death. Finally, the book cast its spell and Esseltine relaxed, closing his eyes to prevent any distraction from the words and for a good half hour all was calm. Then I sprang my trap.

I yelled to the dogs running about the yard as if they were up to no good. They took no notice as I knew they would. My tone was deliberately wrong. Esseltine's eyes shot open, fearful lest he was about to be used as a dog's urinal or even worse, as a dog's supper. I stood and shouted again. I knew Esseltine's eyesight was so poor he would not be able to see in detail what I was so concerned about. In fact, the dogs were behaving beautifully.

"I'm sorry, Mr. Esseltine, for the interruption. The dogs are tearing up the garden. I'll go and get them, put them back in the van. That way we won't be disturbed."

He grunted but seemed pleased that there'd be no wild animals running about his grounds. I went to walk off with Max still in my arms. "Oh," I said, stopping. "Here. You look after Max while I catch the others. I can't run while I'm carrying him."

Before he could object, I thrust poor Max into his unwilling arms. He had no choice but to cradle him or else Max would have fallen to the stone paving. I ran down the lawn to bring the other dogs to heel. I took my sweet time, eventually herding them together to return to the van. I didn't bother confining them because I knew they'd find a spot each and fall asleep from their exercise.

When I made my way back to the terrace, Max was licking the back of one of Esseltine's hands. With his free hand, Esseltine was scratching behind Max's floppy ears or else absent-mindedly petting him. I picked up the book and began reading again watching the two of them bond without the old man realizing it. I read for longer than usual, both because I was enjoying the book and also because Esseltine was more relaxed than I'd seen him in all the months I'd been visiting.

Mrs. Hathaway brought out the afternoon tea, stunned to see Max in her boss's lap. She smiled at me but made no reference to the unusual sight. As we ate sandwiches and drank tea, we discussed Sassoon and his semi-biographical work, while I chose to ignore Esseltine breaking off bits of his afternoon tea to feed to Max who gobbled it from his fingers, his long tongue seeking out any residual crumbs or chicken.

I stood and stretched. "I guess I should head off. Busy day tomorrow. I look forward to discussing the next section of the Sassoon with you."

Esseltine appeared startled, looking to the sleeping bundle on his lap that he'd been petting without thought as we'd been discussing our reading material. I wasn't about to make it easy for him. It had to be his decision.

He opened his mouth to speak. And closed it, obviously gathering his thoughts together. He was a proud man and he needed an excuse, no matter how feeble. I waited. "Look," he said, smiling down at Max. "The little beggar is fast asleep. Seems a shame to wake him." Wouldn't you know it, Max chose that exact moment to wake up and yawn before putting his head back down on Esseltine's lap. I ignored it, waiting for the old man to go on. "Perhaps if you told me what Max needs, I could keep him here until the next time you come to read. That way he gets all the sleep his young body needs. It must have been exhausting for him at the hospital."

"I think I may have something in the van that will suffice. Hold on a minute." I hurried to my van and found two bowls, plus some dry dog food and a few biscuits that would keep Max satisfied until Esseltine could send for other dog food.

"This is for his water," I said placing one of the bowls on the table. "And this is for the dried dog food. I have a big packet here. I'll take them in to Mrs. Hathaway and tell her what she needs to get tomorrow. Is that okay with you?"

"Sure," he mumbled, much too taken with Max to even pay much attention to me.

"But," I emphasized. "No chocolate. Nothing that isn't on the list that I'll give Mrs. Hathaway."

I found Mrs. Hathaway in the kitchen and handed over the bowls. "Max?" she asked. When I nodded, she smiled. "He has no idea how to look after a dog, so I'm relying on you."

"I have two of my own at home. I'll look after him. But it's only until your next visit, isn't it?"

I grinned. She kissed me on the cheek. "You are a clever man, Leon."

Upon my return to the mansion two days later, Max was frolicking on the lawn, chasing a squeaky rubber toy that Esseltine was throwing with obvious delight. "You two seem to have hit it off," I said, slipping into the seat opposite as Max trotted up proudly with the toy between his teeth. When he saw me, he was conflicted as to his loyalties. I gave him instructions via an almost imperceptible nod of my head, so Max happily trotted over to Esseltine, dropping the rubber toy at his feet, to be showered with pats, kisses and exclamations of "Good boy."

Picking up the book, I thumbed my way through the pages. Esseltine cleared his throat. "Would you mind if we neglected the book just for today. No, it has nothing to do with your reading skills or anything like that. It's just such a lovely day, and I don't want to miss a minute of it."

I was about to ask sarcastically whether I would need to add another day to the end of my sentence to make up for it, but I held my tongue, realizing that for many weeks now that I looked forward to my visits and would miss them once they were over. They were the social life I'd been missing.

We sat in silence for a while, Esseltine and Max seemingly content with the repetitive game of fetch. After a while, I wandered off to find Mrs. Hathaway in the kitchen. "He hasn't let that poor dog out of his sight in two days. Do you think it's possible to kill a creature with too much love?"

"It doesn't seem to be doing Max any harm. He is feeding him properly?"

"I thought that would end up being another task added to my list. Not that I mind," she hastened to add. "But, no, he does it all himself. He's like a little kid."

"As long as he doesn't over-feed Max."

"Oh, he's good like that. Measures out the correct amount. Makes sure Max gets his exercise."

I couldn't have been more pleased. When it was almost time to leave, I slid a color brochure across the table to Esseltine. "What's this?" he queried. "My eyesight is not the best."

"I know how much you love your books and I also know how difficult it is for you to read when I'm not here. That shouldn't stop your pleasure. This is a list of audio books from the town library. I can always pick up a few on the way past and drop them in to you. Take them back when you've finished. If there's nothing there that you like, you can order your own from one of the websites."

He looked at me questioningly. "Are you going somewhere, Mr. Paley?"

"No. I'm staying put. I just thought you might like a bit of variety from my monotonous tones."

He laughed. "Anything but monotonous." He pushed the brochure back to me. "Let me hear what's available."

He chose John Buchan's *The Thirty-Nine Steps* and, surprisingly, the first Harry Potter novel. He saw my look when he mentioned it. "I want to see what all the fuss was about. You didn't like it?"

"I loved it," I admitted. "I devoured all the books in the Harry Potter series. It's what turned me on to reading."

"Then, I have to read that."

I packed up ready to leave. Esseltine tensed. He held Max tightly in his lap. "I'll see you the day after tomorrow." I walked away to the van and drove off. I could see the happy smile on the old man's face in the side mirror.

Over the next few weeks, Esseltine became enamored of the new technological marvel of talking books. Well, it was new to him. He devoured them like a man starving. I felt superfluous, and strangely disappointed. I hated sitting about while he chuckled over J.K. Rowling's boy wizard as he grew up.

I'd often wander into the kitchen to chat with Mrs. Hathaway but I still felt redundant. I needed to find something to occupy my time. I found it one day when I walked down the side of the house on my way to the kitchen, only to discover a criminally neglected rose bush attempting to bloom. With Megan's directions I found the old garden tools and set about revitalizing that poor plant.

This in turn led me to really look at the gardens that fronted the mansion, now as dilapidated as the house. I had neither the skills nor the inclination to climb ladders, or test my skills with hammer and nails or paintbrush. I was not built for carpentry. Gardening, however, was kin enough to veterinary skills. I became Esseltine's unofficial part-time gardener. Yes, he did hire someone once a month to keep the lawns to a respectable level, especially now that Max was obviously part of the family.

I dug a garden bed outside the kitchen door, planting herbs that I'd bought with my own money – I still considered I'd got off very lightly considering the amount of damage I'd caused Esseltine initially. Mrs.

Hathaway must have told him about my so-called generosity because, one evening while we were having tea and sandwiches, he handed me a business card for the town's main nursery. "It was very remiss of me not to thank you for all you've done in the gardens. It isn't necessary, you know."

"I rather enjoy it. Getting my hands dirty. It's somehow relaxing."

"I don't want you spending your own money on the upkeep of my property. Anything you need, just go to them." He tapped the card. "It will all be billed to my account."

I started thinking bigger now that my budget stretched a little further. I didn't want to take advantage of his generosity but I did lash out and buy a few well-developed trees and shrubs and had them delivered one Saturday afternoon while I was there. I'd prepared the gardens beside the front door and it was easy enough, with the help of the delivery guys, to slide the new plants into place, fingers crossed that they would be worth the expense and survive. Megan heard the commotion and came out of the house.

"Leon, that's beautiful," she said. "It's beginning to look a little like it did in its heyday when the old house was full of laughter and joy."

I couldn't imagine Esseltine's mausoleum of a house ever being joyful. I'd have to take her word for it.

"It was, you know. When Miss Esseltine was here. Always people coming and going. It was like a madhouse sometimes." She went back inside, shaking her head at the transformation.

The nursery men grumbled at my insistence on their help but left happy after I'd tipped them generously. I was damping down the soil, generally making the plants feel at home when I heard Esseltine grizzling as he was pushed through the house. "Stop shoving me. What's all the fuss about?"

I was still kneeling – I'd learned to wear my oldest clothes by this time – when he reached the front door and had a view of my improvements. "Help me up, Mrs. Hathaway." He wasn't an invalid by any means; he just found it easier to get about in his chair. As she held his arm, he shuffled down the stairs until he stood on the gravel driveway to have a good view of what I'd done.

I was half expecting a query about cost, or some grumpy response, but he merely said, "I'm beginning to think the best thing that ever happened to me was your dog pissing in my slipper." That was the highest compliment I'd ever received from Esseltine. I also took it as his imprimatur to continue. I still had months of my 'community' service to go so I mapped out a plan to transform the gardens as best I could in the time remaining.

The herb garden was flourishing, so it didn't require much attention from me. I must admit to culling quite a bit from time to time to take home for my own use, but it never left the mansion short. My life was so full at that time I barely noticed I was lonely. It hit me most when I went home even though I had the unvarnished appreciation of my menagerie. Trouble was I couldn't take them to bed.

I hadn't been neglecting my duties at the hospital but my relationship with Trish and Bruno had definitely cooled. They suspected I'd become one of Esseltine's allies, though what he could possibly want with my friendship was beyond my comprehension. I merely believed I was paying a debt. If I could make the miserable old bastard a more pleasant human being in the process, then score one for me.

Esseltine asked me if I could transport him to the hospital one weekend as he was due for a check-up. He'd persuaded the doctor to see him on the Saturday as he could get a lift rather than book the local ambulance. Trish put it down to his stinginess and was less than pleased when she discovered that

I was transporting him to the hospital in my van. "Leon, he's already treating you as his personal slave. You really need to put your foot down. It's not right."

The physical exercise I was getting as a gardener had done wonders for my health. I felt better than I had in years. My body was developing muscles in areas I didn't know had muscles so that I now felt comfortable wearing a tank top while I was working in the garden. I had tanned nicely and when the day was not too sunny and the UV reading was low, I'd dare to work stripped to the waist – unless I was working with thorned plants.

Trish couldn't see my new hot body but Bruno whistled his appreciation when he grabbed me by the upper arm to crush me in a bear hug. "Whoa, little dude, is that muscle I feel on your flabby arms?"

I was proud of the way I looked so I flexed for him. "A bit more meat on you and I'll have serious competition." It was a lie – I'd never be as buff as Bruno.

"Where's the miserable old bastard?" Trish asked.

"I left him with the doctor, he'll be along shortly," I said.

"I hope you're taking him straight back."

"Nah, I have to get the pets out to the patients and he said he'd be all right sitting out the back to wait for me."

"Not a good idea, dude," Bruno said. "There's a function on in the private courtyard he uses. He'll have to sit with all the others and with those dogs roaming free…"

I guess they had visions of the old Ralph Esseltine.

"Oh, I think he'll be all right," I said.

Trish sighed. "It's on your head, but I'd hate to see you have to spend another year at his beck and call because one of your pooches shit on his leg."

"My dogs are very well trained," I said, faux indignantly.

Trish and I had been commiserating about our non-existent love life after Bruno went outside to supervise. About twenty minutes later he burst into the office, gesticulating wildly, attempting to catch his breath to croak out, "Come quickly. We're in deep shit." We hurried down the corridor behind him, Trish probably imaging some medical disaster while I had visions of one of my animals injured and in pain. It was neither. When we reached the back entrance everything seemed calm. Except for one yapping little dog.

All eyes were turned in its direction.

"We are so gonna be sued," Bruno whined.

"I don't think so," I said. "Watch."

I knew Esseltine waited until he thought he had everyone's attention. He wasn't a stupid man; he knew his reputation. Once all the attention was focused on him and the barking dog, he slowly lifted his arm and tossed something as far as he could down the manicured lawn. Max took off after his favorite toy, trotting back to Esseltine's side proudly once he'd retrieved it. The old man leaned down and picked up the small dog, settling him in his lap, petting him protectively.

"If you don't close your mouth, Trish, you'll swallow a fly."

She was skeptical at the change. "What have you done, Leon? Spiked his medication with ecstasy?"

"No, it's all his own work. I merely nudged it along with a little help from Max."

"Who's Max?" Bruno asked.

"That's Max in his lap. They're inseparable."

While we watched, Vera Wardrop had one of the nurses move her chair closer to Esseltine. As we went back inside so I could debrief both Trish and Bruno, she struck up an animated conversation with the old man.

By the end of the afternoon, it was agreed that I had wrought a miracle.

My gardening skills were proving less miraculous. A few of the plants died and had to be replaced although the trees on either side of the front entrance flourished. Through trial and error, I learned the parameters of my horticultural knowledge but I was not afraid to ask experts for help when I needed it so my losses became fewer as the weeks rolled on. I was rightfully proud of the work I'd done. I was also pleased with Esseltine's progress. He hobbled around the house now rather than confining himself to the wheelchair. He opened the mansion's heavy drapes to let in more air and light, and had cleaners in to remove what seemed like centuries of dust.

He had not yet committed to repairing the most obvious deterioration but I thought he was getting there. It would be expensive and I knew he'd considered whether the cost outweighed the number of years of pleasure remaining in which he would enjoy it. He had no one to leave it all to. I know it troubled him.

One Sunday afternoon I was working in the gardens that surrounded the driveway in the front of the house. I wanted it to be something special so that when people visited they would get a cheery first impression; a subtle floral indication that things had changed. I was covered in soil, my trousers filthy, my boots coated in mud, my chest and arms streaked with perspiration. It wasn't until a small car drove by that I realized Esseltine had visitors.

I watched as the vehicle, a second-hand Mazda that had seen better days, parked to the side of the front entrance. Two men got out. From a distance they both appeared to be about a decade older than my twenty-eight years. One of them went to the boot and dragged out a pair of suitcases which he dropped on the gravel. I wondered who they were as they gave every appearance of expecting to stay awhile. Of course, it was none of my business although I'd begun to feel slightly proprietorial about Esseltine and his mansion.

Bending my back to my work, I dismissed the two men from my thoughts. I'd find out who they were soon enough. It was about forty minutes until the late afternoon tea Esseltine provided. Deep in concentration I must have missed the fact one of the men was calling for my attention. It was only after an ear-piercing whistle that I looked up. "Are you deaf?" he called indignantly. "I've been shouting at you for absolute ages."

I stood still and stared at him. There was something about the man that raised my hackles. "Don't just stand there. Come over here when I'm talking to you."

The gravel crunched underfoot as I made my way up the path to where they were standing. The man who had called to me appeared flustered and angry. "Take your time, we have all day." He was a sarcastic bastard.

"What can I do for you?" I asked.

"For starters you can address me as 'sir.' Then you can put a shirt on, you're a disgrace. And then you can take our bags inside and wait for instructions on which room to take them to."

I took the sweat rag from my back pocket and mopped my brow. I looked the man up and down. He was not unpleasant on the eye although his friend was much more to my taste. "What are those things attached to your shoulders?" I asked politely.

The man's brow furrowed. "Arms?"

I nodded. "What's that at the end of your arms?"

"Hands," he retorted.

"Are you disabled in some way?"

"Of course not."

"Then carry your own bloody bags," I snapped. Turning to walk back to the garden, I paused a moment before adding, "I call no man 'sir,' unless he has earned my respect. You have a long, long way to go before that will ever happen." I headed back to my work.

"I'll have your job for that," he shouted after me.

The second man tried to calm his friend. "Don't fuss, Geoffrey. We can carry our own bags, for heaven's sake. It's not the end of the world."

"The hired help should know their place," Geoffrey huffed.

I kneeled down in the garden, pretending to be preoccupied with one of the plants while I was, in reality, watching the two interlopers. They went to the front door and rang. I watched as Mrs. Hathaway greeted them, inviting them inside. Just before he disappeared, the better looking of the two turned to look at me. It did things to my body and my prick – things I hadn't felt for so long I'd forgotten what lust felt like.

My supposition that the prodigal grandson was paying a visit was confirmed a little later after I'd cleaned up as best I could to join Esseltine on the terrace. I was still a bit of a mess but that's a given with hard manual labor. Or manual labor that you're not used to.

"Ah, here he is now," Esseltine said as I approached. Two sets of eyes turned in my direction. One pair seemed surprised but amused; the other was so like a storm I expected lightning bolts to strike me dead. There was no point antagonizing them further. When Esseltine proudly announced, "This is Rohan, my grandson," the old man sounded so proud and so pleased, my hand shot out automatically toward the twat who'd been so insulting. The fruit had not fallen far from the tree in that family.

"No, I'm Rohan," a deep sexy voice said. I turned to the second man who grasped my extended hand and shook it warmly. "It's nice to meet you, Leon."

"Likewise," I stuttered.

"This is Geoffrey, a friend of mine," he added.

Geoffrey took my hand but it was cold and dead to the touch, then grunted a greeting. I didn't bother grunting back.

We sat down again and the sandwiches and tea were served. Geoffrey screwed up his nose. "I don't much care for tea." He turned to Mrs. Hathaway. "I'll have a soy latte and…" he picked the top off one of the sandwiches, "Urgh. White bread. No thanks. Some skinned chicken on multi-grain bread, no butter. And certainly none of this yellow muck that you've drowned it in."

Esseltine looked at the young man like he had two heads. Rohan laid his hand on his friend's wrist, speaking softly. "This is not a restaurant, Geoffrey. Drink your tea and eat your sandwich." I was so jealous of that wrist. I wanted Rohan's hand on mine.

Geoffrey went to object but one glare from Rohan and he capitulated. Rohan took two sandwiches to compensate for his friend, and then turned to me with his megawatt smile. "Geoffrey has something to say to you, Leon." I could listen to him say my name all day.

Geoffrey choked on the small piece of chicken he'd managed to extract from between the slices of bread, scraping off the chutney. It was telling that none of us slapped him on the back to help dislodge the morsel. Once he'd regained his composure, still a little red in the face, we all waited. Geoffrey cleared his throat ostentatiously as if to imply he had almost choked to death. "Ah…um…I would like to apologize for my behavior earlier today. My only excuse is that you looked like one of the staff."

It was the most miserable apology I'd ever heard. Geoffrey was about to wipe his fingers on a napkin but Max, who'd been listening to the conversation from under the table, struck first, flicking out his tongue to lick Geoffrey's fingers. "Oh, good Lord," he shrieked. "That animal licked me. Now I'm all covered in germs. I think I shall be sick."

I offered the dog a larger piece of chicken to get him out of harm's way and he trotted over to my side. Esseltine and Rohan noticed while Geoffrey continued his rant. "I shall have to go to my room and shower. I'm allergic to unclean things," he declared.

Mrs. Hathaway led him away. I'm sure she was using all her willpower to stop herself from laughing. Once they'd gone inside, Rohan visibly relaxed. "I'm sorry for my friend. He can be a drama queen sometimes."

We ate and drank our tea in silence, all staring at something in the distance that seemed to require the utmost concentration. I was silent because I found I was so attracted to Rohan I could scarcely control my dick. It threatened to burst out of my trousers it was so hard. If he was gay, and I wasn't sure of that, then Geoffrey was probably his boyfriend. Geoffrey might be an asswipe but I didn't get involved with guys already in a relationship. I wouldn't like being cheated on, so I wouldn't do it to others.

Rohan put his cup down – Megan had brought out a new set of china cups for the occasion – and stood. "I had best go check on him. If you'll excuse me."

I watched him walk off. Again, he turned to look at me as he got to the door. I gave him what I considered my most winning smile. I'd scarcely gone back to my sandwich when Esseltine, his face puckered like a lemon, said, "Do you think they're fags?"

I sighed. "Mr. Esseltine, it's not my place to gossip about other people. Besides, that term is so totally offensive I don't think I should even be sitting at the same table when you speak like that."

He seemed genuinely surprised. "Like what?"

"The word 'fags.' It's offensive."

"Only to fags," he said. He must have thought about it for a moment because he looked at me, his mouth agape, his eyes open wide. "Mr. Paley, you're not…" He didn't know what word to use.

"Yes, Mr. Esseltine. I am. Just for your information, you may call me gay, homosexual, or even queer. Never fag."

"I never would have guessed," he mumbled.

"If it's a problem."

"No. No, it's not. I've known my fair share in the business world. They usually married and had children. Tried to fit in."

"I'm not one to attempt to shoe-horn my gay life into a pretend straight relationship."

"Do you have a young man?"

"Not for a while."

"Are you looking or are you one of those promiscuous homosexuals?"

"I'm still looking."

"I hear there are some places you can legally get married now." He shook his head. "In my day, they'd just lock you up or send you off to a mental institution."

"We've come a long way since your day," I laughed.

"Mm, it's probably all for the best." He thought about it for a while. "Do you think they are?"

"Probably."

"You think my grandson is doing it with that Geoffrey character?"

"I don't know," I said.

"I hope not," Esseltine spat. "If he is then his taste's in his ass, just like his mother's."

I looked at him, wondering whether the expression had been a slip of the tongue or whether he'd been deliberately provocative. "What?" he asked. He must have thought about what he'd said because he began to giggle, attempting to hold it back, but that just made it more difficult, and soon we were both laughing so heartily my eyes were watering.

Of course, Rohan walked out of the house at that precise moment. "What's so funny?"

"Private joke," I wheezed.

"Mr. Paley, would you mind pushing me inside. I think all this excitement has been a bit too much. Rohan, I'm so glad to have you here. I know it's not easy and there's a long, painful road ahead but I hope we can get to be friends."

"Me, too, grandfather."

I picked up Max and placed him in Esseltine's lap before I pushed him toward the house. Rohan said, almost as an afterthought, "I hope you're coming back."

I was coy. "If you like."

"I would like very much."

"I'll ask Mrs. Hathaway for a fresh pot and some more sandwiches."

"That would be good."

Safely inside, Esseltine looked at me strangely as I strapped him and his chair onto the Inclinator. "You like him, don't you?"

I blushed. "Mr. Esseltine."

"Now that I know about you, it's obvious. What about that nurse Bruno at the hospital? I've seen him hug you."

"We're good friends. He's totally straight. He's bedded most of the nurses."

Esseltine chuckled. "A boy after my own heart. When I was young, before I met young Rohan's grandmother and settled down – I was never unfaithful to her once in all the years we were together – I was quite the tom cat."

He was still smiling at the memories as I pressed the button and he began his ascent. I found Mrs. Hathaway muttering to herself about Geoffrey. "That Rohan seems a decent enough sort but his friend..."

I agreed. After asking if she'd mind making a fresh brew and a few more of her delicious sandwiches, I made my way back outside. Rohan hadn't disappeared as I thought he might.

"Megan is bringing the tea," I said as I flopped down in my seat. "Mrs. Hathaway."

"Good." He looked as if he wanted to say something but obviously thought better of it before he finally asked. "If you're not the hired gardener, what are you doing here?"

I didn't think he meant it rudely, so I was happy to respond. "It's a long story. And a very strange one."

"Everything associated with my grandfather seems to be a little strange. For instance, I was told he was the most insufferable old bugger ever born. He's a bit of a curmudgeon maybe, but that's about all."

"It really is an awfully long story."

"I don't mind a bit. Geoffrey is in one of his shitty moods and I'd rather be anywhere but sharing a room with him."

My heart sank. That was the answer I least wanted to hear to the unasked question.. I told my story as expeditiously as I could, Rohan interrupting a few times but only for clarification. Mid-way through my story, Mrs. Hathaway brought more sandwiches as well as a new pot of tea and a few delicious European biscuits she saved for special occasions. I looked at her as if to ask what the occasion was. I was taken aback when she winked and nodded her head in Rohan's direction. I suspected Esseltine had something to do with it.

When I'd finished the story, Rohan chuckled. "So, you brought about my grandfather's total transformation single-handed."

"I can't take all the credit. I merely set it all in motion. Max did the rest."

He held up his tea cup as a toast. "Here's to Max. Long may he thrive."

"Amen," I said, raising my cup. "May I ask your story?"

"It's even longer than yours, but much less colorful. For the moment, suffice it to say, my grandfather's letter finally tracked me down at a time my life was at its lowest ebb. His invitation to come and stay with him here in Callicoma was fortuitous. My company had just gone bust; I'd lost my apartment, and my car. I don't usually drive a second-hand Mazda that was lucky to make it here. I must admit, my reasons for accepting the invitation had less to do with the suggested rapprochement and more to do with my grandfather's wealth. I'd heard the old man was incredibly wealthy and also incredibly ill – near death, in fact – so I thought…well, you can imagine what I thought."

"You are his next of kin."

"That doesn't excuse my wishing the old man dead. Or at least, remorseful enough about the way he'd treated my parents to settle a large sum on me in exchange for my forgiveness. Besides, I had no idea if he'd fathered more children. I knew nothing about my mother's side of the family, apart from the rather one-sided portrait my mother painted."

"What sort of business were you in?"

"Finance. What else? It's where you go to make the largest amount of money in the shortest amount of time with a minimum of your own capital. Geoffrey talked me into it. I opened my own firm with the money my mother left me but I hated everything about the business. It was such a relief when the financial sector collapsed taking my firm with it, even though it left me without a penny."

"What would you like to do instead?"

"I'm afraid I'm a very practical person. I'm not good with abstract concepts like numbers and stock markets and futures and all that shit. Besides, I don't like to take advantage of people simply because they're greedy. I much prefer to do something to help people."

"Are you good at anything?"

"That's the problem, I don't know."

"How about you come and help me with the gardens next time I'm here."

"As long as you don't blame me if the plants all end up dead."

"It takes a lot to kill a plant. Think of your interaction with the trees and shrubs and flowers as like a relationship. It's easiest to kill them off through neglect."

"Are you cynical because of a bad experience in the past?"

"What?"

"Don't tell me my gaydar is wrong. I'm sorry, I thought you were gay. Please forgive my flirting with you. I'm such an idiot."

"No, I'm gay," I said. "Wait, you're flirting with me?"

"You really are out of practice, aren't you?

"Not much to flirt with in a small town like this."

"Geoffrey thinks you're flirting with my grandfather to get your hands on his money." I spat my coffee across the table, barely missing him. "Yes, I thought he had hold of the wrong end of the stick. Grandfather strikes me as an old-fashioned homophobe, not someone who would react well to a cute young man flirting with him."

"If you lay on any more compliments I'll begin to think you like me. And, yes, I think your grandfather has a few issues, but he's learning. Those biscuits you're eating. Only for special occasions. I think he and Mrs. Hathaway may be playing cupid."

"We only met each other a few hours ago."

"And you have a boyfriend," I added.

He sounded surprised. "Do I? Oh, you mean Geoffrey?" I nodded. "Been there, done that, got the scars and the empty bank account to prove it. It was short-lived. Geoffrey has a terminal case of promiscuity. He can't bear to let any good man go without trying it on. He succeeded far too many times for my liking."

"One time would be one too many for me. But he seems very possessive, if you don't mind my saying so."

"I don't mind what you say. I'm rather past caring what other people think. He would like to rekindle what we had, but what we had was not what I wanted. I'm a pretty conventional white picket fence, a cat and a dog sort of guy."

"And Geoffrey hates animals?"

"Yes, another reason we're an unsuitable match. Now you, being a vet…"

"Why is he here with you?"

"Honestly? He smelled money. Lots of money. Geoffrey's like a sniffer dog in that regard; he can smell cash a hundred miles away. And the scent of cash was all over grandfather Esseltine's letter. He insisted he come with me because he knows how to negotiate the best outcome."

"For himself."

"And for me. But I mainly needed a friend to be with me when I met the man whose invisible presence so dominated my mother's life. I had no idea what to expect. I'm a bit of a coward really."

"No, I understand. I think I'd feel the same way."

Rohan yawned. "Much as I would love to spend more time talking to you, it's been a long and exhausting day. And I have an emotionally draining day tomorrow with grandfather. I want to be open and honest with him, so I don't know what will happen. He may throw us out."

"I hope not."

"Me, too." We both stood and he ran his fingers down the side of my face. I leaned in to kiss them. He pulled me to him and kissed my cheek. Then planted a kiss on my lips although he kept his mouth closed. It was enough. For now.

I went home elated.

The next two days couldn't go quickly enough. I was frantic to see Rohan again. It was like a drug. I didn't believe in love at first sight; it was a ludicrous concept. No, I was horny. Perhaps Rohan and I were just hot for each other's bodies and our ardor would cool once we got it out of our system. Fat chance. In my case, my attack of the lusts was because I'd put my social life on hold for months because I was so busy paying off my debt to Esseltine. In fact, I hadn't given sex much thought lately, so the first cute man comes along and I fall apart. I wasn't sure that Rohan's flirting meant anything other than he fancied a quick bedroom romp and then an equally speedy departure. Well, I could handle that. Or so I tried to convince myself.

Fortunately for my mental wellbeing, Rohan was still at the mansion when I returned. He was waiting for me dressed in cut-off jeans that molded his perfect ass. He also wore a muscle T-shirt that strained to contain his body, a body that I wanted to throw on the paving stones and ravage. Esseltine seemed to show a keen interest in our chatter.

"Going somewhere?" I asked with raised eyebrows.

"Is that offer still open about helping you out?"

"Of course."

"There'll be no ordering Mr. Paley about, Rohan. He's in charge."

"I think you might be confusing me with Geoffrey, grandfather."

"Indeed, I might be."

I retrieved the tools from the shed at the back of the house, the shed upon which I had imposed some semblance of organization. Rohan helped carry them to the garden on which I'd been working when he first arrived.

I couldn't help myself. "You look so hot dressed like that. I want to throw you down in the dirt and have my way with you."

"I'd enjoy that," he smirked.

"But your grandfather is watching. I suspect, too, that Geoffrey is watching us from behind his curtains in the upstairs bedroom..."

"No need to worry about Geoffrey. He had urgent business to attend to in town."

"Oh? He will be back though?"

"Once the swelling and his black eye go down."

"My, he is persistent."

"That included attempting to climb into my bed in the middle of the night. Now I lock my door."

I didn't want to talk about Geoffrey. That just put me in a bad mood. "How did it go with your grandfather yesterday?" I showed him where to dig and we talked, developing a rhythm together.

"Both better and worse than I expected."

"How?"

"He's quite happy for me to stay here sponging off him for as long as I like. In fact, he encouraged it. He's not prepared to buy me off. Nor is he prepared to die suddenly so that I may inherit. That last one was a joke, by the way."

"I thought it might be. So, what have you decided?"

"I can't just sponge off the old man. It's not in my nature. But I have no money and no prospects to move on to, not without he stakes me. I thought about getting a job in the town but there's not much doing for someone without qualifications."

"You could always spend time in the gardens when I'm not here, considering I can only work on it a few hours every other day. On top of that, Mr. Esseltine still likes to hear me read to him from time to time even though he has his talking books. It would be great for the gardens and a big help to me. My, um, 'community' service, as I like to call it, is due to run out in a few months. Of course, I'd like to continue but I don't know how Mr. Esseltine feels about that."

"I can tell you. We spent more time talking about you yesterday than about me. I think you've become the surrogate grandson."

"I'm sorry. I never intended that."

"There's nothing to apologize for. The two of us have a lot of catching up to do. A lot of fences to mend. It may take some time. I'm not sure I have the energy."

"Don't be so defeatist."

"I think he's waiting for me to prove myself."

"He thinks you came back for your inheritance?"

"That would be my guess. Of course, Geoffrey's behavior didn't help dispel that idea. Grandfather caught him examining the family silver. Took his notebook away from him and found his calculations on how much many of the items in the house were worth. It wasn't a good look."

"Ouch."

"Ouch is right. I think I went one step forward and three steps back in my grandfather's estimation."

"Only by association."

It was great having Rohan help me, not least because we got the work done in record time. We'd turned the soil and broke up the thick clay clods, ready for fertilizing and then planting.

We rested for a while to get our breath back. Rohan leaned against the shovel to survey the front of the house. "Is that your work?"

"Yeah."

"It's pretty good," he said.

"Especially if you'd seen what it was like before."

"Mind if I make a suggestion."

"No, go right ahead. I'd be happy for constructive input. I'm no expert. I don't pretend to be."

He wasn't pushy, he merely pointed out areas for improvement, playing down his ideas almost as if they weren't really worth considering. I didn't agree with all of them, mainly based on financial considerations, but I listened and he did have a couple of wonderful suggestions. In fact, some of them were downright genius.

"Come with me." I was so enthusiastic I dragged him along behind me toward his grandfather who was in his usual spot on the terrace, a large umbrella above him to protect him from the sun's rays. He had the buds in his ears listening to his latest audio book which I continued to pick up from the library although he was in danger of having heard almost the entire stock. He'd tentatively asked me to sound out the librarian about whether they would be prepared to accept a donation of any such books if he bought his own and had no further need of them.

Once the librarian had got over the shock of Esseltine showing generosity, she was enthusiastic about his offer, especially as the library was chronically under-funded. She gave me a list of requested books which they were too strapped for funds to buy, suggesting that I might persuade Esseltine to add one or two of those to his list of self-purchases. Once I'd explained to him about the request he asked me to order everything on the list and have it sent to the library as an anonymous donation. Then he proceeded to tell me which books he wanted. It was also quite a list and it would keep him in material for months.

I coughed to attract his attention because he liked to listen with his eyes closed while he stroked Max who was in danger of becoming too large to sit on his lap.

He didn't hear me so I put my hand on his shoulder. He paused his machine. "Is something the matter?"

"Go on, tell him your ideas," I encouraged.

"Well, they're not totally my ideas. You had a lot of input, refining my more outrageous flights of fancy," he said, bumping against my shoulder.

"Don't be modest."

In the end, Rohan explained his vision, for a vision it was, for the driveway. To that point I had been cobbling together a garden in an ad hoc manner. My exertions were because I felt beholden to the man for the damage I'd caused.

Esseltine listened carefully to Rohan's suggestion, nodding from time to time. Then he asked the most pertinent question of all. "Who is going to undertake all this back-breaking work?"

"We will," Rohan and I chorused.

Esseltine merely smiled. Placing the buds back in his ears, we were dismissed to get on with turning the dream into reality. Rohan brought out the best in me when we worked and I seemed to do the same to him. I was surprised, for example, when I returned two days later to discover that he'd drawn sketches of his ideas. Yes, they were rough but they were works of art in their own right. His list of improvements even included general repairs to the outside of the house. They were little more than basic carpentry repairs, cleaning out the eaves, and a bit of paint, but it was impressive what could be achieved on a budget.

"Have you shown these to your grandfather?" I asked.

"Nah, it's just a bit of scribble."

I grabbed his shoulders, forcing him to look me in the eye. "Don't sell yourself short, Rohan. These drawings are amazing. Truly. You have a real skill." He looked pleased at my praise. "Come on, let's show him."

"I'd rather you didn't," he replied.

"Why?"

"He might think I'm interfering. Trying to take over. Muscle in for when he dies."

"Okay. I take your point."

"Why don't you tell him they're yours?"

"I'm not taking credit for someone else's work."

He wore me down throughout the remainder of our afternoon together so that while he was cleaning up, I took the plans to Esseltine. I laid them out on the table before explaining what they meant, although it was self-evident.

"Rohan do these?" he asked.

I nodded. "He asked me not to tell you in case you thought he had an ulterior motive."

"Do you think he has?"

"I'm not the world's greatest judge of character, but he appears sincere to me. He wanted me to take credit for these but I couldn't do it."

"I like them, Mr. Paley. No offence to you, but I like them even more since they came from my grandson."

"I quite understand. No offence taken. In fact, I would like to suggest that I relinquish control and hand it over to Rohan. He's here all the time so he can make decisions without having to refer to me. It will make the process speedier."

"Well, you two discuss it among yourselves and let me know your decision. That's very generous of you, Mr. Paley."

It took a bit of persuading but eventually Rohan saw the sense in his taking control. "I'll always ask your opinion, Leon. I'm an amateur."

"You're streets ahead of me. Anyway, animals are my first love. Flora comes a poor second."

Over the next few weeks, Rohan persuaded me up a ladder to clean the gutters which were clogged with what looked like centuries of leaves and nests. We also painted the trimmings once they'd been cleared of cobwebs, and replaced some of the rotting woodwork. Rohan proved adept at carpentry. I was hopeless. I couldn't even hammer in a nail straight. Working with Rohan was fun. The only thing that spoiled it was

Geoffrey's flying visits. He'd found himself a job in a prestigious financial house, happy to commit small investor's savings to dubious get-rich schemes while skimming off a substantial commission for himself. He attempted to convince Rohan to join him but his pleas fell on deaf ears.

He was always disruptive when he arrived, laying waste to our equanimity, making unreasonable demands on our patience and time. We got much less achieved when he was in residence. Things came to a head on one such visit when Esseltine had us all around the table for the tea and sandwiches ritual. "I just wanted to say a few things today because I've been watching everyone at work. I've spoken to Mrs. Hathaway privately but what I have to say here concerns you all. Firstly, I never thought I would see the old house looking so spruce. Yes, I know we've merely glossed over some more serious problems but I've decided to spend a bit of money to get the necessary repairs done."

"Hold on a minute," Geoffrey interrupted. "You can't just go ahead and make unilateral decisions like that."

Esseltine's eyes narrowed. I knew to leave well enough alone when that happened. Geoffrey sailed on blithely unaware. "As Rohan is your next-of-kin, I would have thought you'd consult him before you spent any of his money."

Rohan looked on horrified at the onrushing car crash.

"His money?" Esseltine bellowed, frightening Max who jumped down from his lap and hid between my legs. This was the old form Esseltine. I was glad it was aimed at Geoffrey and not at me as it had been in times past. Rohan looked to me as if to query whether this was Esseltine of old. I nodded my head. Fasten your seatbelts, it's gonna be a bumpy ride.

"Well, it will be. Soon as you drop off the twig. And that time is fast approaching. After all, you're not a young man. Why else do you think he'd be wasting his time in this godforsaken hole? You don't honestly believe he actually likes it here." He went off into gales of hysterical laughter as if that proved his point.

Esseltine appeared gutted. "Is that true?"

Rohan merely looked sheepish and lowered his head.

I couldn't stand it any longer. "Stand up for yourself, Rohan. Tell him it isn't true."

"He can't, because it is true," Geoffrey spat, his saliva like a snake's poison.

Esseltine called to Mrs. Hathaway who had come out onto the terrace to see what the commotion was all about. "Bring me my check book, please."

We all remained silent while we waited for her return. I wondered what was going on. When she came back, Esseltine quickly scribbled out an amount for cash that made my hair curl. It was more money than I'd make in a decade. He handed it to Rohan. To no one's surprise, Geoffrey snatched it, sneered at the amount, before adding, "You're getting off the hook very cheaply, old man. If it was me, I'd sue you for every penny in your miserly bank account. You owe him."

Rohan bustled him away. He was still muttering as they went inside. Esseltine looked totally destroyed. "The bank will ring about it. Will you cancel it then?" Mrs. Hathaway asked.

Esseltine's response was a simple. "No." He asked to be taken to his bedroom. Before he left, he said to me. "Mr. Paley. You have proven an invaluable friend to me for which I am exceedingly grateful. If only you had been my grandson, I would be a proud man today. I absolve you of any further need to repay your debt to me. In fact, this very day I have deposited what I consider a very fair amount to cover your time and expenses as you worked on my house." I went to interject. "I know, I know. You didn't do it for the money but I believe in a fair day's wage for a fair day's work. Please accept it with my thanks."

"May I come back and finish the job. You don't have to pay me, Mr. Esseltine."

"Ralph, the name is Ralph. But I don't think so, Leon. I don't really think so. I never thanked you for your precious gift, Leon. I am so appreciative of Max. I could never repay you for the pleasure he has brought into my life. I'll cherish him and take care of him. If I should die before Max does, I'm sure you'll find him a good home for the remainder of his years."

"I'll look after him myself." I was on the verge of tears. Geoffrey had torn down all the good that had been done over the past nine or ten months. I couldn't stand to see Esseltine so crushed.

"After Leon leaves, and my grandson and his companion are gone, please bolt the doors so no one can get in, Mrs. Hathaway. I desire some time alone."

I gave them time to get upstairs before I strode determinedly into the house and up the stairs, bursting into Rohan's room as he packed. "What the hell do you think you're doing?"

"You know I couldn't lie about why I was here. I admitted that what Geoffrey was saying was the truth when we met. There's no future for me here. I belong with Geoffrey. That's the sort of people we are."

"I don't fuckin' believe you," I screamed. I shook him but he made no attempt to resist. I pulled him to me and kissed him hard, forcing my tongue between his lips. It took time but eventually he reacted, kissing me back. I ran my hands down his body, gripping his ass to pull him tighter against me until I felt the outline of his hard prick pressing against mine. I broke for breath. "What about us?" I asked.

"What about us?"

"Don't tell me you don't feel it. I can't sleep for thinking about you. I want to rush over here on my off days just to see you, just to hear your voice. It's been agony for weeks working with you when all I want to do is kiss you, feel your naked body wrapped in my arms. I see the way you look at me. I know you want it as badly as I do. Please stay, Rohan. We can work something out."

"Yes, I do feel for you, Leon. But it scares me. I've never cared this deeply about anything before."

"Then stay. Stay with me. Your grandfather will come around eventually."

"I don't care about his money. It was just nice to have family for a change. I was really getting to like him. I hoped he was getting to like me."

"I'm sure he was."

"But he doesn't trust me. Can't say I blame him after the poison Geoffrey sprayed."

I shut his mouth with another kiss. I wanted to prove how much I liked him. I hoped it would be enough to make him stay. It wasn't. All I could do was stand and watch as a triumphant Geoffrey led him away. I humiliated myself by calling after them, "I love you, Rohan." My declaration was met with a peal of sarcastic laughter from Geoffrey.

I packed up my van and drove home; feeling like my world had ended. Suddenly the prospect of endless nights with nothing to occupy me but the memory of what might have been with Rohan stretched ahead and I didn't like it. It was still only mid-afternoon. I had been taking more and more time off my veterinary chores to spend time with him, always leaving my cell phone number taped to my surgery door for emergencies. There was rarely anything that couldn't wait until the next morning.

To make up for it now I spent time with my pets, they always made me feel better but even they weren't doing the trick that day. I gave them clean water and food. They hadn't been neglected even though I'd spent more and more of my spare time up at the mansion. I suspected though that Esseltine – Ralph – was going to feel very much alone and neglected in the weeks to come. Of course, I would try to remain in contact, even attempt to complete Rohan's dream; I just had no idea of how amenable the old man would be to my interference.

I watched a bit of television with Tynan resting his head on my thigh. Whatever the program was, it wasn't sinking in. I went to bed early, too distraught to stay up any longer. Fortunately, my troubled dreams were interrupted by loud knocking. It took a little while to realize the sounds were coming from the front door of the surgery rather than inside my head. I got up and wrapped my robe around me. I hoped it wasn't a real emergency because I was not in the mood.

"I'm coming," I shouted as the caller was getting impatient. I looked through the security peep hole but I couldn't make out the face in the darkness. I unlocked the door and opened it. "Rohan? What are you doing here?"

He'd been drinking. "I did it, Leon. I finally did it."

"Did what?"

"I told Geoffrey to piss off. To never come near me again."

"Come in. Don't stand outside in the cold."

"I thought you'd never ask," he said, stumbling over the step into my arms. I took advantage of the situation, planting my mouth against his, forcing him to react. He tasted of bourbon and triumph. There would be time enough to ask him what happened after I'd got my fill of his kisses.

We broke apart. "I could really go a strong coffee," he said. "And maybe something to eat."

"I don't run a restaurant," I said, an echo of Rohan's words to Geoffrey on that fateful first day we met. "But how about scrambled eggs and bacon?"

"Yeah, I guess it's almost time for breakfast."

Rohan followed me into the kitchen, seating himself at my small table while I got the ingredients together. "So, tell me what happened."

"Geoffrey drove straight to the bank. It was about to close but he insisted we were there on behalf of Ralph Esseltine. That got their attention and they couldn't do enough for us. I thought when they rang the mansion to confirm the check was genuine that grandfather might deny us the money. He didn't. The things you said to me kept running around in my head and while I watched Geoffrey order people around as if they were his personal serfs, I guess I snapped. They weren't getting the cash together fast enough for him. I told him a small-town bank was unlikely to have enough ready cash but he wanted it as soon as possible so that if there were any problems he could march right back to the mansion and have it out with my grandfather. In the end, they could only raise around twenty thousand. I told Geoffrey to take it and go; that I would follow the next day after bank gave me the remainder.

"He looked at the pile of cash on the counter. Greed got the better of him. I knew he was only after me for the money he thought he could make. In the end, he piled the notes into a carry bag the manager had his groceries in. 'You won't come after me tomorrow, will you?' I decided to be honest for a change. 'No, Geoffrey. This is goodbye. I'm paying you off to leave me alone. I never want to see you again. Is that understood?' 'Oh, babe,' he moaned, 'we could have been so rich.' 'We want different things,' I said. He smirked. 'You want that gardener?' That brought it home to me. I'd been happier in your company than I ever had been in my life before. I felt as if I belonged, really belonged. Once I accepted that, it was easy to say goodbye to Geoffrey forever, even though he'd been my only friend. I told the bank to put the rest of the money back in my grandfather's account, keeping just enough to tide me over in case I had to sleep on the streets."

"How did you find me?"

"Easy. I remembered the name of your practice, *Creature Comforts*. All I had to do was look you up. I still have my cell phone. And here I am."

I slid the plate of fluffy scrambled eggs and crispy slices of bacon across the table and then pulled up a chair beside him. I had two forks and we both helped ourselves from the one plate. It was the most intimate thing we'd ever done. We couldn't stop smiling at each other.

"What are your plans for the future?" I asked once the meal was finished.

"I was hoping your invitation still stood."

"Which invitation was that?"

"About staying here with you."

"For how long? Just the night?"

"Longer."

"A week?"

"Longer."

"A month?"

"Nuh. Longer."

"It'll be mighty cramped. And the sofa bed is very uncomfortable."

"I'm not sleeping on the sofa bed."

"You're not?"

"I'm sleeping in your bed."

"Where am I sleeping?"

"Next to me."

I dragged him down the hallway to the bedroom. Tynan didn't look at all pleased to be hunted out of the room and the door closed in his face. He'd be okay; he'd make himself at home on the sofa. I pushed Rohan onto the bed, sprawling on top of him, lips locked upon lips, the feel of hard cocks in our trousers pressing against each other.

"This is not sleeping," Rohan smirked.

"Is that what you want to do?"

"Does it feel like it?"

"Unless you have a flashlight stuffed down the front of your pants, then no," I said.

"Flatterer."

"Come on." I helped him off the bed and slowly unbuttoned his shirt, rubbing my hand across his smooth chest, tweaking his nipples.

"I'm not too old for you?"

I looked him up and down. "Just how old are you?"

"Thirty-five."

"Oh, grandpa, you are so the man I've been looking for."

He was startled. "Exactly how old are you?"

"Twenty-eight. And a half."

"Still a spring chicken."

"Are we going to talk all night. Or…"

"I prefer the 'or.' Here, let me help you."

We tugged and tussled at each other's clothes, taking longer than we would have had we undressed ourselves, but our way was definitely sexier. Finally, we stood in our underwear. He wore the tightest briefs that hugged his body revealing exactly how excited he was. He was chunky, the way I like my men, with very little excess fat. I could have done with a little hair on his fine chest but nobody's perfect although Rohan was the closest thing to Heaven I'd ever had in my bedroom.

My boxers looked daggy in comparison although they did nothing to hide my arousal either. Taking a deep breath, he dropped the briefs and stood naked, shyly awaiting my approval. I whistled. "You're gorgeous."

I don't know why, but he blushed, jumping into bed to cover his nakedness. "Shy as well," I added.

"Come on, let me see," he said impatiently.

I did a pretend strip tease, slowly peeling one side of my boxers down, then the other. He had a peek of my trimmed pubic hair before I turned around and slowly revealed my ass cheeks. I heard moans from the bed. Then my underwear was down around my ankles and I kicked them aside. "Turn around."

As instructed, I turned and his groan got louder. "Please tell me you have all the necessaries."

I went to the night stand and found the condoms and lube, placing them under my pillow. "I lived in hope."

He fished them out and examined them. "These are new."

"Uh huh."

"You bought these in the hopes that I…?"

"You're embarrassing me," I squealed.

"That's the sexiest damn thing I've ever heard."

That was enough talking. I pulled him to me, wrapping my arms around his warm body, kissing his neck, nibbling his skin. Moving lower, I ran my hands across his chest before sucking each nipple in turn which made him writhe in the bed, attempting to push his hardness against my body. I licked my way down his belly until I felt his heat against my cheek. I was in a teasing mood and lapped at his balls rather than taste his cock. "You're torturing me," he complained.

It was torture for me too, so I relented and ran my tongue across his oozing slit. I wanted to make this last. He tried to force his prick into my mouth but I held him back. "Not so fast," I murmured. I ran my tongue around the head, placing my lips gently against the skin. Weighing my skills up against the length and thickness of his beautiful cock, and judging that he was close, I pushed my mouth down and down until I felt him hit my throat. I paused and bobbed up again, suctioning against his shaft. He called out my name. I had him.

I picked up speed as I plunged down again, taking him into my throat this time, manipulating my muscles to give him extra pleasure. "Fuck, Leon. What you're doing to me." I kept my head in position for as long as my breath held, then repeated the process over and over, memorizing the feel of his cock in my mouth in case I never got this opportunity again.

I wanted so much to have this man, increasing the speed, increasing the pressure, until I felt a clutch in his balls and his cum spurted into my throat. I pulled back and his taste was on my tongue. I swallowed all he had to give me before I licked him clean. He lay there panting when I moved up beside him. Unlike some men who will never kiss once you've had their spunk in your mouth, Rohan had his tongue between my lips even more passionately than before.

He pulled me on top of him so that I lay between his legs, my prick throbbing against his body. He raised his knees which was all the hint I needed. I reached for the lube to squirt some on my fingers. Parting his cheeks I found his hole and began to push one of my fingers into the steamy opening. He felt so good but I didn't want to rush things. I gave him time to adjust to one finger before adding a second and, finally, a third. I told him to sheath my cock. Ripping open the foil packet with his teeth, he rolled the condom down my cock before I lubed it. I pulled his feet against my chest to give me better access to his anus, rubbing the head of my cock up and down before aiming for the bullseye. I pressed slowly and his muscles gave. I watched the head of my prick slowly engulfed by his sphincter. I was inside.

He relaxed before I pushed in deeper. He slapped my butt in encouragement and I sank in the rest of the way in one stroke, my balls slapping against his ass. "That feels so good," he hissed. Beginning with slow, smooth strokes, I moved positions until his gasp revealed I'd hit his pleasure spot. I didn't want him to come just yet so I massaged it with my cock every other stroke. "You're killing me," he moaned.

"But what a way to go," I replied.

Once he got used to my thrusts, I picked up speed. "That's it, baby," he muttered. "I like it hard." That would be my pleasure. I lifted off my knees, slamming my cock into his ass, hard enough to move his body up the bed. He encouraged me with dirty talk, something none of my previous lovers had ever done. I liked it. "You have the most fuckable ass in the world, Rohan. You were meant to have cock inside you."

With the friction and the dirty talk, it wasn't long before I was squirting my love inside him as he held my butt to keep me locked in place. One last thrust and I was done. I eased out gently and then lowered his legs to the bed before peeling off the rubber to drop it in the bin beside the bed. Rohan grabbed me, tucking my body in front of his, spooning me. "I thought I was supposed to do that?" I said.

Rohan nudged his stiff cock against my butt. "I'm not one for stereotypical roles. I like to be versatile."

"Pleased to hear it," I murmured. "So do I. Just not right at the moment though. I'm buggered."

"No, I thought that was me."

We both laughed but exhaustion overtook us both and, moments before I fell asleep, I heard a light snore from behind me. It was the early hours of the morning when I awoke, an insistent prick prodding at my butt cheeks. "So, you didn't sneak out during the night?"

"I haven't had my turn yet."

"I hope this is not going to develop into a competition."

"Not if you pass me a condom."

"How can I refuse when you ask so nicely?"

Rohan topped me this time and there were no complaints from either side. It had been a while for me so he took it easy and I enjoyed the leisurely pace which he picked up as he reached orgasm. My cock was hard but it's never been easy for me to come while being fucked, even when I'm jerking my own dick. Rohan took care of me afterwards, his oral technique equal to his anal skills.

In the afterglow, the time in which some people like to smoke, we used it to get a handle on, well, everything.

I went first. "Are you staying?"

"Do you want me to?"

"Of course, I do."

We circled the subject of our relationship, neither of us willing to be the first to commit in case it scared the other. In case it was too soon. I was the first to get jack of it. I grabbed his face and held his eye while I said, "Stop pissing in the wind. I'm looking for a relationship. I like you, really like you. I think we could be good together. I'd like to give it a try."

"Way to put pressure on a guy," he said, but I could tell he was joking. He turned serious. "I'm penniless, no place to stay, no prospects, no skills…"

"On the positive side. You have a lovely cock, and an ass that needs servicing on a regular basis."

"That's not enough though, is it?"

"No, not in the long-term," I admitted. "But you can stay here. It's not much. You can help me around the vet clinic, it's almost getting to be too much for one person now anyway. You can help muck out the kennels, do handyman shit. You're good at that. If you want, you can look around for other jobs at the same time." I had an idea what was troubling him. "And we can try to get your grandfather back onside."

"It's not about the money."

"I know."

"I really got to like him."

"There's a good man underneath all that curmud-geonliness."

"Is that even a word?"

"It is now."

We showered together, avoiding temptation by a mere whisker. We had a simple breakfast of grilled cheese and baked beans on toast, and tea. I had animals to feed and exercise, patients to see. I opened the surgery early because Vera Wardrop was already perched outside with Sherlock.

"It's good to see you, Vera. Sherlock all right?" I asked as I ushered her into the waiting room.

She was breathless. "Have you heard about old man Esseltine? Kicked out his grandson. Seems he was a gold-digger."

"Did you come here to gossip or does Sherlock have a problem?"

Rohan took that moment to come out into the waiting room. "Is there anything I can do to help?"

Vera looked from me to Rohan and back again. She must have read something in our faces. "Oh," she squeaked.

"Yes, 'Oh.' Now I know it's no use asking you to keep it a secret for the moment because you're one of the biggest gossips in town—" She huffed indignantly. "Don't try to deny it."

"So, are you two…you know…"

I turned to Rohan. "Are we?"

He shrugged. "I guess we are."

Vera kissed me on the cheek. "Thank goodness. You've been lonely for so long."

She attacked Rohan and kissed him as well.

"Trish Nolan owes me twenty dollars."

I was confused. "What?"

"The whole nursing home was taking bets," she grinned. "Odds were 75/1 you'd never get it on. 10/1 you do the nasty once or twice and then split up. It was 100/1 that you'd really get it together and…you know… settle down."

"It's early days yet," I said.

"I can see it in your eyes. You can't disguise that, no matter how hard you try. Come on, Sherlock. We have news to spread." She bustled toward the front door. "Congratulations. I couldn't be happier. And, Rohan. He'll come round. Just give him time." Then she was gone.

I went to cuddle him. "She spreads news faster than a virus. The whole town will know before lunch. Do you mind?"

"Nah. Saves me having to come out. What about you? Do you mind?"

"Hell, no. I'm proud to call you boyfriend."

"Just one thing."

That made me nervous. "Yeah."

"Are we exclusive?"

"I hope so," I replied.

He breathed easier. "Good. That's the way I like it." He kissed me to seal the deal. "Now, what can I do?"

"How about you be my receptionist for the day. Everyone is going to want to meet you so we might as well have you front and center. You could get patient files out and put them in order in that basket there. Saves me time and any arguments about who was here first."

Rohan was flabbergasted. "You have paper files? It's not all on computer?"

"I was going to get around to it. I have been busy you know."

The morning went by comparatively easily. Rohan's handling of the patients eased my workload more than I would have thought. A few patients, those lucky (or unlucky) enough to be on Vera Wardrop's bush telegraph, asked whether Rohan was my new man. I confirmed it with pride, hoping I wasn't hexing the relationship with a premature announcement. By midday the waiting room was empty.

"What now, boss?" Rohan asked.

I was annoyed. "I'm not your boss, you're my partner."

He looked pleased that I said that but, at the same time, chastened because I'd snapped at him. I put my hand on his shoulder. I saw a few sketches on his reception desk. "What's this?"

He snatched them away before I could pick them up. "It's nothing."

"What are you hiding?"

"It's nothing. Really."

"It's a bit early in our relationship to be hiding things, isn't it?"

That did the trick. Reluctantly, he handed over three sketches. It was the waiting room. The best that could be said of it in it's then current state was that it was functional. Rohan had sketched three views of an alternative design. "These are amazing, Rohan," I said.

"You're not upset?"

"Why would I be?"

"My first morning and already I'm telling you how to rearrange things."

"If all your ideas are as amazing as this, then don't hold back."

He was delighted. "Really?"

"Yeah, really. Just keep in mind the cost."

"I think I could pretty much do this on my own. I'd only need help with electricals and plumbing."

"Okay then. What are you waiting for? Get planning. I'll get you a credit card linked to mine and you can buy what you need. Just let me know so I can balance the books with the accountant."

That took his breath away. "You'd trust me with your bank details?"

"Why wouldn't I?"

"After everything I've told you?"

"Rohan, love. There's not enough cash in my account to get you to the state border."

I was exaggerating but I wanted to put him at ease.

"Thanks, Leon. You are one helluva guy."

I rang the bank to organize an ATM card while Rohan measured up the waiting room in between patients in the afternoon. He'd been given the third degree all day by people wanting to know if he was Esseltine's grandson, what the old bastard was like, and was he now the vet's boyfriend? I would have been irritated by the questions but he fielded them with good humor winning a lot of admirers in the process. He won my admiration by not slagging off about Esseltine. He accepted full responsibility for the estrangement.

It was just about closing time when the door flew open and Trish stormed in. "What's this I hear about you and Esseltine's…" She stopped when she saw Rohan behind the reception desk. I was going over his plans for the renovation with him. "So, it's true." She had her hands on her hips, demanding an explanation.

"We were going to tell you first but Vera got the drop on us and we were up to our asses in patients. You know how it is. Are we forgiven?"

"He's too old for you," Trish snorted.

Rohan was indignant. "I'm only eight years older than Leon."

"He's feisty," she said. "How about you take me out for dinner. Then I'll forgive you."

"Why not?" I said. "Rohan, show Trish the plans for the surgery."

I went out to lock up and feed those animals that needed fresh water or their kibble topped up. When I returned, Trish was utterly enthralled by Rohan's vision for improvements. "I wish we could do something like this at the hospital," she complained.

"Why can't you?" he asked.

"Lack of funds. Lack of will on the part of the Board. Maybe one day."

The meal went off without a hitch. It took a while for Trish to warm to Rohan who mounted a charm offensive. Maybe he tried a little too hard, but by the end of the evening, she gave her tick of approval. In fact, that seemed to be most people's attitude. A few homophobes muttered about sin and civilization headed for damnation but, for the most part, people seemed to be pleased for our relationship. Rohan became a feature of the reception area as well as helping me on weekends at the hospital.

There was a black spot in our lives, however. Esseltine wouldn't take our calls; neither mine nor Rohan's. Megan nodded sadly when I went to the house but she refused to allow me inside, apologizing that it was her job if she disobeyed. I couldn't think of any other way to get through to Esseltine. The letter that I'd written had been returned unopened.

It was a constant irritant but we were so busy that we thought about it less and less as time went on. My new waiting room – it took three eighteen-hour days over a public holiday weekend – impressed the hell out of everyone, especially when Rohan owned up to doing it himself (with a smidgen of help from me – I supplied the coffee and pastries). People began asking him to do small jobs around their homes and he was happy to oblige. He never took payment so people gave in kind. We received preserves, jams, cakes, pies, produce, almost to the extent we didn't have to go shopping. Rohan was careful not to impinge on the work of local carpenters. If the job was large, he referred people to the experts, but the simple things he did himself.

But it was his design skills that attracted attention. He had no background in the business and couldn't draw up a plan to scale to save his life but his ideas, they were works of genius. Trish even had him sketch ideas for the hospital but, inevitably, as she predicted they were knocked back.

The first weekend we went to the hospital as a couple, Bruno bailed us up in the yard. "So, you're the dude that's won the heart of my little buddy?" He poked Rohan in the chest and scooped me beside him with his muscular arms. "I've had my eye on him for years now." Rohan looked stricken, probably weighing up his chances beside this giant muscle god. "I was just waiting until my gay hormones kicked in, then I was gonna ask Leon to marry me."

I giggled. "Bruno, you don't have a single gay hormone in your entire body. You're so straight, you can't even bend over to pick up the soap."

He let me go. "You wound me, Leon."

"Get over it," I laughed.

"Come here, dude," he said to Rohan. He pulled us into a group hug, kissing us both on the forehead. "I couldn't be happier. You take good care of my little buddy, Rohan. Or I'll be coming after you. Make sure I get an invitation to the wedding."

"He's intense," Rohan said after Bruno headed off to help one of the patients.

"Biggest heart in the universe," I replied. "And his cock comes a close second."

"Now you have me intrigued. How do you know?"

"All the female nurses say so."

"No personal experience, eh?"

"He really is so straight he puts an arrow to shame."

Our lives settled into a regular pattern which some people might think of as monotonous or boring – it was anything but. My affection for Rohan deepened by the day. We'd never discussed the future, I think we both assumed it would go on as it was. The sex was still incredible although I think in the over-all tally, Rohan bottomed more than I did. His choice, not mine.

He kept his odd jobs to a minimum because he got more pleasure out of his sketches. One morning, we were visited at the surgery by Mike Parker, one of the local tradesmen. I thought at first he was there to complain about Rohan taking away his business. Rather, he unfolded one of Rohan's sketches, asking, "Are you responsible for this?"

Rohan acknowledged it was his drawing.

"I'm getting a lot of these from clients. How much are you charging them?"

Rohan was shocked. "I do it for free."

"Then you're an idiot, son."

"Hold on," I interrupted.

"No, you hold on. Rohan is it? You could be making good money if you come and work for me."

"I'm not a draughtsman," he said. "I just see things in my head."

"I could use someone like you in my firm."

"You'd charge a packet to the client for my ideas, wouldn't you?"

"That's how we make money."

"I don't think I'm interested."

"Your loss, sonny." He turned to leave. "Hold on, you're not in cahoots with Tony Mercer, are you?"

Mercer was one of the town's other carpenters and builders in competition with Parker.

"I'm not in anyone's pocket, Mr. Parker."

Parker seemed quite pissed off at this stage. "Suit yourself." He strode to the door in a temper.

"Mr. Parker," I called. "Leave your card. I think we might be able to do business. Just give us a few days. Is that all right with you?"

"At least one of you talks sense," he muttered as he removed a card from his wallet and placed it on the counter. "Don't take too long about it. And don't try playing me off against the others in the town."

"Didn't like him at all," Rohan said once Parker had left. "Pushy little bastard. I wouldn't last five minutes working for someone like that."

I nodded. "No social skills at all." I did, however, agree with Parker on one point. I didn't think Rohan should be giving his ideas away. Some people who could afford professionals to do the design work were approaching Rohan in expectation of free designs which they then took to architects and professional builders and landscapers.

"I like working here with you," Rohan pleaded when I told him of my idea. "Besides, I'm only half-way through putting your old files on computer."

I had to admit that was a monumental help which I would have had to pay someone big bucks to do otherwise.

"I'm not being lazy, Leon. I do want to work but there's tons to do around here for the moment. I guess I'm not really a nine-to-five office type."

"I know, love." I thought about it for a moment. "Well, if you don't want to work for one of the building companies, what about you work for all of them?"

"I haven't got a head for business, you know that. Look at what a failure I was in the past."

"And look at you now." I pleaded and cajoled for a short while before he gave in.

"Okay, what's your idea?"

Rohan listened and the more I talked the more interested he became until he could scarcely sit still in his chair. "That might just work. Why don't we give it a go?"

It took a bit of organizing but we booked the large meeting room at the town library – they were more than happy to help considering the number of talking books that I'd delivered from Esseltine – and even more cajoling to get the local builders, landscapers, architects, anyone at all who might find Rohan's sketches useful, to attend on the same evening. We laid on a light supper which Mrs. Hathaway was happy to prepare although she had no better news about a rapprochement between us and Esseltine. He'd gone back to his reclusive ways although he still listened to his novels, and Max was still his constant companion. "But it's not the same as when you were there," she admitted.

Of course, few of the people who attended the meeting were enthusiastic at first. "That's communism," Parker yelled when we posited the idea.

"Look," Rohan said, finally finding his balls. "I don't want to work for any of you…businesspeople full-time. Do you get it? I'm not a nine-to-five office type.

I don't want to have to answer to anyone. But I do want to keep doing my designs. If I have to, I'll do them for free." There was uproar from the meeting. "But I would prefer to make a little money. It helps pay for groceries."

"Look, what's not to like about this idea? You all stand to make money from it," I added.

There was some grumbling, particularly from those who would have preferred to be the sole company making a profit out of Rohan. Smaller firms were delighted with our idea.

"Anyone who's interested in signing up, please see Rohan after the meeting. You others, well, the offer is always open." In the end, most of them signed up rather than miss out. Self-interest always wins in the end. Rohan would continue to do his sketches for zilch but would advise prospective clients that if they took them to one of the recommended tradespeople in his attached brochure there would be a slight surcharge that would come back to him in exchange for which he would be available for onsite adjustments to the plan. He would liaise all along the line without it costing them an arm and a leg.

It was slow to take off but once businesses saw an increase in trade, it snowballed. Parker, naturally, was the last to sign to Rohan's 'socialist agenda.' Our income increased, meaning we were more comfortable, but hardly wealthy. Rohan kept an eye on charges and a few construction companies had to be warned off their exorbitant extra fee for Rohan's services, but they backed off.

The only fly in our ointment was Esseltine. We had no idea how to get him back onside. He had his pride and it would not allow him to even contemplate our friendship. It was Trish that finally had an idea.

"He's coming in for a check-up next Saturday," she said at dinner, something we did once a month now. "We offered him an alternate date because he knows you're there with the pets on that day. That leads me to believe he's half expecting to run into you."

"I agree," I said.

"What's your plan?" Rohan asked.

"That's it," Trish said.

"That's not a plan," he complained.

"I'm giving you advance warning so you can come up with your own ideas. I'm an administrator not a fucking introduction agency."

"I'll think of something," I said to calm the waters.

In the event, I had one feeble idea that I wasn't sure would work. I didn't want to tell Rohan about it because it would either open the door back into Esseltine's life, which we both wanted, or it would bolt the door forever. I could only give it my best shot.

The Saturday morning was sunny, for which I gave thanks, so Esseltine was seated in his wheelchair on the lawn, Max sleeping beside him. He had his ear buds in, listening to one of his books. We let the animals out, the dogs heading off straight away while the cats much preferred to preen themselves before bothering with their duties. I guess they wanted to look their best. Rohan and I delivered the less perambulatory creatures to the wards.

When we were back at the van there was one dog still remaining. Rohan smiled. He'd guessed what I was about to do. "Do you think it will work?"

"I'm hoping."

Rohan swept me into his arms to kiss me passionately.

We were seen. "Dude, that was so hot, I think I might be turning gay after all," Bruno called as he escorted a patient to the terrace.

Rohan ignored him. Instead he turned to me. "I love you so much, Leon Paley

I was flabbergasted. "You used the 'L' word."

Rohan smiled. "I did, didn't I?"

"We'll discuss that when we get home. But just FYI, Rohan. I love you, too. I have for a long time."

I lifted the doggy box from the back of the van and opened it. I patted the dog, cooing instructions in his ear, my heart beating fit to burst. "Go boy. Do your duty. Make us proud."

The dog shot off at high speed, heading straight for its target as Rohan and I watched from the side. Esseltine was startled by the speed at which it attacked and, true to his old form, he attempted to kick at it but his legs got caught in the blanket constricting him. Bruno had incapacitated the unsuspecting Esseltine in his chair. He'd also lured Max away with the promise of a treat, so the old man was vulnerable.

"Get away from me, you bastard."

Tynan managed to get up close and personal, lifted his leg and pissed over Esseltine's expensive slippers. The old man bellowed, "I'll get you for this, Leon Paley. It'll be years before you pay this off." I noticed he was attempting to stop a smile.

"Good boy, Tynan," I said when the dog trotted back looking very pleased with himself. I fed him a treat.

Rohan and I high-fived. It looked as if everything was going to be all right after all.

Lydian Press

ABOUT THE AUTHOR

Barry Lowe writes about love and sex so he won't forget how to do it. When he's not scribbling his adventures for the Sydney gay weekly *SX¸* or out doing field research, he's writing about love's wonderful variations for a series of smut eBooks, novels and anthologies for Lydian Press

 Go to www.barrylowe.info

OTHER WORKS BY BARRY LOWE

Available in eBook and Print

PLAYS

THE DEATH OF PETER PAN: Gay Historical Romance

NOVELS & ANTHOLOGIES

BUSTING BILLY'S BUTT: A Gay Erotic Romance
Steve and Billy's monogamous relationship has gone stale until Billy, ever the exhibitionist, shows them a way to spice up their sex life.

THE MAJOR AND THE MINERS: A Gay Historical Romance
1930s Australia: Two men from opposite ends of the social spectrum. Is love enough to overcome the obstacles between them?

THE GRAVY TRAIN: A Murder Mystery with Recipes
Someone on the train has an appetite for murder!

A TOUCH OF THE SON: A Gay Novel
Their secret passion will lead them to hell. Will they be able to find their way back?

ROMANCING THE BONE: Gay Romance Erotica

OMG! NOT ANOTHER GAY EROTICA ANTHOLOGY?

ROUGH & READY: Gay Tough Guy Erotica

YOUR BOYFRIEND IS HOT: Gay Cuckold Erotica

BEAR SKIN: Hot Gay Bear Erotica

THE MORE THE MERRIER: Gay Gangbang Erotica

THE BOY IS A BOTTOM: Gay Anal Erotica

COCK-EYED OPTIMISTS: Gay Romance Erotica

BABY, I'M NOT A MONSTER: Gay Vampire and Other Paranormal Erotica

CHRISTMAS CRACKER: Gay Erotica for the Holidays

BUTT BOYS: Gay Anal Erotica

SELECTED SHORT FICTION
Available as eBooks

SUMMER AT RAINBOW COVE

I WAS A MALE NYMPHO FOR THE FBI

THE DAY OF THE CLIFFORDS

HE WON'T SEND ROSES

A RED ROSE BEFORE CRYING

PRIDE AND JOY

ROAD HUMP

THE GOOD, THE BAD, AND THE CUDDLY

THE GROOM CLOSET

TUNNEL VISION

HARD ON HIS HEELS

SPIN THE BOTTOM

THE NEW DAD'S CLUB

FOUR ON THE FLOOR

TAGGED BY THE TEAM

WANNA SHARE YOUR HUSBAND

For all Barry's titles please visit his page at:

lydianpress.com

Lydian Press is dedicated to bringing you the finest GLBTQ erotic literature on the web.

Visit us on the web at:

http://lydianpress.com

www.ingramcontent.com/pod-product-compliance
Lightning Source LLC
Chambersburg PA
CBHW060936050726
47592CB00003B/981